"I kiss

"I noticed. And unless Wes had lost all his powers of observation, Ingrid might want it to happen again, whether she'd admit it or not.

"But I shouldn't have." Her color was high.

"Why not?"

"Because I just broke up with my boyfriend. He cheated."

Ouch. "How long ago did you break up?"

"Three weeks."

"Three weeks?" That wasn't very long. No wonder her emotional reactions were topsy-turvy. "Is he in town?"

"He's in Boston."

"Ah."

"The point is, I'm kind of a mess right now."

"I can understand that." Unfortunately, she was also tempting as hell.

She looked at him with her Caribbean blue eyes. "Could we just forget about that kiss?"

Not on your life. "I'll do my best."

A COWBOY'S CHALLENGE

THE MCGAVIN BROTHERS

Vicki Lewis Thompson

Ocean Dance Press

A COWBOY'S CHALLENGE
© 2018 Vicki Lewis Thompson

ISBN: 978-1-946759-51-1

Ocean Dance Press LLC
PO Box 69901
Oro Valley, AZ 85737

This is a work of fiction. Any resemblance to actual persons, living or dead, business establishments, events, or locales is entirely coincidental.

Cover art by Kristin Bryant

Visit the author's website at
VickiLewisThompson.com

1

Attention, Eagles Nesters!

Wes Sawyer untangled himself from the covers and staggered out of bed. What the hell?

Cut the chit-chat, folks, and sign in at the parade registration table! That means you!

Ah. It was just Ellie Mae Stockton on her bullhorn, organizing the Fourth of July Parade. He flopped back onto the bed. He didn't have to...oh, wait. He'd promised his brother Pete he'd be in the thing. Grabbing his phone, he checked the time. Yikes.

But he couldn't go down there without a shower. Savoring the aroma of freshly baked bread and pastries wafting up from Pie in the Sky, he walked into the bathroom. His sister Roxanne's old apartment wasn't modern or fancy, but its location above the bakery was primo. When she'd asked him to take over the lease he'd jumped at the chance.

He twisted both knobs of the ancient shower. A tiny stream of water dribbled out. Damn it! He was fragrant after all those sweaty hours helping a client's mare through a difficult labor. A sponge bath wouldn't do it. Now what?

Assuming Ingrid's shower worked, he could ask to borrow hers. She'd be downstairs making specialty coffee drinks and baking up a storm, but he could call her.

No, he couldn't because he didn't have her number. Her apartment would be unlocked because nobody locked doors up here, but he couldn't use her shower without permission.

Cussing a blue streak, he tugged on the clothes he'd left in a pile when he'd dragged himself home at four this morning. He'd totally spaced the parade. Pete, responsible oldest brother that he was, would be in the staging area, checked in and waiting for him.

He picked up his phone as he went out the door and called Pete. "Hey, bro. I overslept."

"You'll be here, though, right? Fudge and Clifford are saddled and ready to go. Roxanne came over last night and did a little mane and tail braiding for us, too."

"Nice. Listen, I'll come as soon as I can. I hope we're toward the back of the parade."

"Yeah, sort of. Just hurry."

"I will." He disconnected the call as he got to the bottom of the stairs. Twisting the deadbolt, he stepped into pre-parade chaos. Main Street had been blocked off for vehicles but it was packed with chattering people, whinnying horses, high school band kids testing their instruments and a float that had stalled on its way to the staging area.

"*Eagles Nesters!*" Ellie Mae climbed up on the stalled float, bullhorn in hand. Her blinged-out jeans and fringed vest glittered in the sun. "*Some of you still haven't signed in! Make your way to the sign-in table immediately!"*

Wes threaded his way through the noisy crowd to the bakery's front door. It stood open and the line stretched a block down the sidewalk. He approached the door and touched the arm of a middle-aged woman standing in the opening. "I'd appreciate if you'd let me get by, ma'am. I'm not going to order anything. I just need a word with someone in there."

The woman glanced at him. "Who?"

"Ingrid Lindstrom. She works here."

"It's sardine city in there, son. You'll never get to her. "

His height allowed him a decent view of the interior and sure enough, it was a sea of customers. Ingrid had to be in there, but where?

"You could borrow Ellie Mae's bullhorn." The woman chuckled as if she'd made a joke.

"Good idea." Moving as quickly as possible without shoving, Wes reached the side of the float and made a megaphone of his hands. "Miss Stockton!"

She turned and walked to the edge of the float. "I remember you! You're one of those good-looking Sawyer men. Spokane's loss is our gain."

"Thank you, ma'am. Can I borrow your bullhorn for about thirty seconds?"

"Promise you'll bring it right back?"

"Absolutely."

"Well, all right. Wouldn't normally do it except you're cuter'n a bug's ear." She handed it down.

"Thanks, ma'am." He worked his way back to the bakery's open door and raised the bullhorn. *"Ingrid, it's Wes! Can I use your shower?"*

All the chatter stopped and everyone stared at him. He hadn't counted on that.

"Yes!" Ingrid shouted back. Her laughter was drowned out by everyone else's.

Okay, so he'd made a fool of himself. He was in too much of a hurry to care. After returning the bullhorn to Ellie Mae, he dashed up the stairs. He snagged a towel and washcloth from his bathroom before jogging the length of the hall to Ingrid's apartment. He'd been in it once briefly to borrow matches for his gas stove but he'd been too busy to socialize.

On opening the door, he was greeted by a colorful poster that hadn't been there the first time. He would have noticed a cartoon of a cycling fish. *A woman needs a man like a fish needs a bicycle.*

He chuckled. Having a sister had taught him a fair amount about women. A smartass poster like this didn't appear for no reason. Likely some guy had ticked off Ingrid, and recently, too.

Locating the bathroom was easy. He just followed his nose to the lemony scent he associated with her. Add in the warm pastry smell she picked up at work and she was an aromatic delight.

Stripping down, he turned on the water, picked up his washcloth and climbed in. Her setup was like his, a small glass enclosure that probably suited her fine. He usually banged an elbow or knee at least once during every shower.

Maybe he should have brought his own soap and shampoo. Didn't think of it. After this he'd smell just as lemony as she did. He'd find some way to thank her for the use of her stuff.

He was racing the clock, but he wiped down the walls of the shower and mopped up the floor with his towel. He'd never mastered the art of getting out and drying off without dripping, especially in this tiny space.

Wrapping the towel around his hips, he scooped up his clothes and hot-footed it back down the hall. Following a quick shave, he put on his nicest Western shirt, dark blue with some silver embroidery on the yoke. If Fudge was stylin' with a braided mane and tail, a classy shirt was the least he could do.

His jeans weren't new but they were clean. He gave his boots a once-over with his bath towel before shoving his feet into them. Wallet, door key, cell phone, hat. He was outta there.

Taking the stairs two at a time, he went outside, locked up after himself and pocketed the key. He let his hair dry in the breeze instead of putting on his hat right away. While he'd been upstairs, Ellie Mae had restored order, which was a very good thing. The parade was five minutes from kickoff.

As he passed the bakery's front door, Ingrid turned the hanging Open sign to Closed. She gave him a quick grin and a thumbs-up. He returned the gesture. The goodies in the bakery's window made his stomach growl, though.

Nothing to be done about that, now. He headed to the end of the street where two guys on horseback stood waiting for the signal to start the parade.

Wes had lived in Eagles Nest less than a month, so he was still learning who was who. But there was no mistaking Ryker McGavin and Badger Calhoun, both dressed in Air Force blues and holding flags that rippled in the breeze. He smiled and lifted a hand in greeting.

"Cuttin' it a little close, there, Wes," Badger called out.

"I'm aware of that, Badger." He lengthened his stride as he moved down the line. He passed the ENHS marching band in their green and gold uniforms, lined up and ready to play Sousa, no doubt. Next were the vintage cars and trucks, most sporting patriotic flags or bunting.

Faith, who'd married Cody McGavin a couple of months ago, was driving her green pickup with the Whine and Cheese Club in the back practicing their dance routine to *Born in the USA.*

"Get a move on, cowboy!" Kendra McGavin called out.

"What she said!" Wes's dad grinned at him from the seat of his vintage Harley positioned behind Faith's classic truck. "Glad you could make it, son."

"I'm not there, yet, Dad." He was a little surprised that Kendra was with her girlfriends instead of sitting on the back of his dad's bike, since they were crazy about each other.

Then again, they'd warned their kids this would be a non-traditional love story. For one thing, they didn't intend to live together. His dad had sold his place in Spokane so he could be with her, but he'd bought horse property across the road from her ranch.

Despite the buzz of voices and hum of idling engines, Ellie Mae's voice came through loud and clear on the bullhorn. "*It's time! Move 'em out!*"

As the band struck up *Stars and Stripes Forever*, Wes jammed his hat on and jogged past an elaborate float for Zane McGavin's birds of prey rescue organization, Raptor's Rise. A precision drill team that had at least two McGavin brothers in it followed behind the float.

Beyond the drill team, Roxanne waved to him from the Guzzling Grizzly float. She was perched on a bar stool next to her fiancé Michael Murphy. The country duo that had helped put the GG on the map—Bryce McGavin and Nicole Williams—tuned their guitars.

The GG float edged forward. Pete was right behind it, mounted on his big roan Clifford and holding Fudge's reins. "About time."

"Sorry." Wes took the reins and swung into the saddle.

"At least you made it."

"Barely." He tapped Fudge with his heels and they started off at a slow walk behind the float. "Thanks for trailering my horse over here."

"Had to. He's been asking about you."

"I'll bet." He reached down and stroked the gelding's silky neck. "Sorry to be AWOL, Fudge. Love the red, white and blue ribbons, buddy."

"Roxanne outdid herself. Figured it was our first parade and all. How come you overslept?"

"Had a foaling last night. It ran long."

"How much shuteye did you get?"

"Three hours, maybe a little more."

"Ouch."

"Can't complain. Business is good."

"If it doesn't kill you."

"Hey, this is what I asked for." Wes glanced over at his brother, who looked more like their dad every day. Pete had inherited the Sawyer coloring of light hair and eyes, while the rest of them took after their mom.

Pete grinned at him. "As they say, be careful what you ask for."

"It'll settle down after a while. I'm grateful to Kendra for talking me up. She's a one-woman promo team."

"Tell me about it. The foreman job she recommended me for is working out great."

"That's good to hear. I haven't seen you since you started working there."

"I noticed. Dad and I had this crazy idea if you based your practice in Eagles Nest, the Sawyer men would get to hang out, have a beer together now and then."

"Like I said, it'll taper off. Kendra will run out of leads. But are you okay being foreman of a ranch that isn't yours and Dad's?"

"Love it. I can ask for days off. I draw a paycheck instead of wondering if we can meet payroll when our income dips. I can't speak for Dad, but ever since we sold the Lazy S, I've felt like somebody lifted a Brahma bull off my shoulders."

"I'm happy for you. I—oh, there's Ingrid." She'd come outside to stand on the sidewalk with

Abigail, the owner of Pie in the Sky. As luck would have it, they were on his side of the street. He'd have an opportunity to thank her. "I had to use her shower this morning."

"Say what?"

"Old building, dicey plumbing." He admired the way sunlight picked out the golden highlights in Ingrid's hair. She'd worn it in a ponytail today.

"Good thing you had a shower backup, then."

"Amen to that. I was ripe."

"Whereas now you smell like lemon drops."

"You can smell it way over there?"

"The breeze is in my direction."

"Trust me, it's an improvement from how disgusting I was earlier." The GG float stopped and Wes drew back on Fudge's reins. Perfect. He was exactly opposite Ingrid. He smiled at her and tipped his hat. "Much obliged for the loan of your shower."

She smiled back. "No problem."

"Are you going down to the park?"

"Wouldn't miss it."

"Great." He turned to Abigail. "How about you?"

"Definitely. After the parade's over, Luke's coming back to fetch me."

"With his truck?"

She laughed. "On his horse, believe it or not."

"Great idea. Gives me one." He slipped his left foot out of the stirrup and held out his right hand to Ingrid. "Hop on and I'll give you a lift."

"Oh, that's not necess—"

"Come on." He beckoned with his hand. "It'll be more fun than walking."

"Parade's moving, bro," Pete said.

"It's now or never, Ingrid."

"Okay, why not?" Taking his hand, she put her foot in the stirrup and grabbed the cantle as she swung up behind him. "Yee-haw!"

"Hold onto me."

"Gotcha." She wrapped her arms around his middle.

The nearness of her warm body plus the aroma of lemons and baked goods gave him a sensory high. "We're off." He touched Fudge's flanks with his heels. Best idea ever.

2

Until the moment she'd wrapped her arms around Wes, Ingrid had placed him in two categories—older brother of her best friend and new neighbor down the hall. They'd exchanged casual greetings on the stairs and sat at the same big table when a group gathered for dinner at the Guzzling Grizzly. She'd thought nothing of letting him use her shower this morning.

But sitting behind him on his magnificent horse was an entirely different experience. She'd swear he hadn't been this solid when he'd visited Roxanne back in March. He must have been lifting weights. Even though they'd been living in the same building for the past month, she'd somehow missed the fact that he'd muscled up.

Impossible to ignore it today. His broad shoulders radiated strength. How inconvenient. She didn't want to notice his physique—or any man's for that matter. Not after the way Mark the cheating jerk had ground her heart into the pavement.

She'd just have to put it out of her mind. She could ride down to the park with him without being affected. Joining the parade had sounded like fun, and she was determined to enjoy the experience. She and Abigail had talked about creating a float for Pie in the Sky but that would have meant closing the bakery on parade day and losing a ton of revenue.

"I didn't think to ask if you'd ever been on a horse." The rumble of his voice was rich and smooth, like a well-made latte.

She'd ignore that, too. "I have. I rode with my friends when I was a kid." She glanced over at his brother. "Hi, Pete."

"Good to see you, Ingrid." He touched two fingers to the brim of his Stetson.

"Kendra says you and your dad are settling into your new place."

"We are. It needs a few more renovations, but taking care of it will be a cinch after the Lazy S. Eventually we'll have room for Wes if he ever decides to move out of that apartment."

"Thanks, but that won't be happening." Wes was relaxed in the saddle, his left hand holding the reins and his right resting on his thigh. "I wake up in the morning and smell delicious things baking and amazing coffee brewing. I'm only steps away from food and drink fit for the gods. Why would I give that up to batch it with you guys?"

"I take it that's a no."

"That's a hell, no. But that reminds me. I'm starving. Will there be food at the park?"

"You bet," Ingrid said. "I'm hungry, too. The diner sets up a food tent and serves meals and snacks from mid-morning to mid-afternoon. The GG takes over after that."

"Meaning I could get pancakes this morning?"

"Pancakes, scrambled eggs, bacon, sau—"

"Stop." He groaned. "You're killing me."

Pete chuckled. "Wes can eat."

"Nothing wrong with that." She appreciated a good appetite. If people didn't like to eat, she wouldn't have a job, let alone a promising career.

On the GG float ahead of them, Nicole and Bryce launched into one of their original songs, which was a treat but made conversation difficult. Ingrid smiled and waved at people she knew along the route. So did Wes and Pete, although being new in town they weren't recognized as often as she was.

Riding behind Wes, she had an intimate view of the back of his neck, which was slightly sunburned. His dark hair didn't curl as much as Roxanne's but it was just as thick and lustrous.

She shouldn't be noticing that, either, but she was a sucker for good hair. She'd loved running her fingers through Mark's, especially after they'd made love. On her surprise visit to Boston three weeks ago, he'd come to the door with his hair rumpled. Then she'd discovered why.

That memory did the trick. She stopped focusing on Wes's hair. After Nicole and Bryce finished their number, she grabbed onto a neutral conversational topic. "This is a beautiful horse, Wes. Is he yours?"

"He is, although I wouldn't be surprised if he disowned me. I haven't spent much time with him since I left for school. This is Fudge."

"Is he named that because he's sweet or because of his coloring?"

"Both. I got him when I was sixteen. Some kids get cars at that age but we all got horses."

"Well, he's very handsome." She glanced over at Pete. "So is yours."

"Thank you."

"What's his name?"

"Clifford."

"Like the big red dog in the kids' book?"

"Exactly."

"Clifford and Fudge. Two good names. Original and easy to remember."

"We get no credit for them," Wes said. "They were already named when we got them." He turned and flashed a grin at Pete. "I seem to remember you hated the name Clifford."

"Pretty much, but I wasn't going to change it and confuse the poor guy."

"Well, I read that book when I was little," Ingrid said. "And I like Clifford's name. I like Fudge's, too. His coat is just the right color. Who did the braiding with the ribbons?"

"Roxanne," Wes said.

"Figures."

"She insisted on it," Pete said. "She used to do it for fun when we were all at the Lazy S. Didn't need an occasion. She was thrilled that Fudge and Clifford would be in the parade this morning and that we'd be riding behind the GG float."

Ingrid laughed. "I'll bet she was. I keep forgetting she wasn't here for this last year, either. It seems I've known her forever."

"She feels the same way about you and Abigail," Wes said. "Like she has sisters, now."

"That's me, too. I—" She didn't finish as Nicole and Bryce hit the first chords of another song.

When it ended, Wes glanced over his shoulder at her. "What else goes on at the park today besides eating?"

"You name it. Tug of war, three-legged races, water balloon faceoff, horseshoe tournament, pie-eating contest—"

"Your pies?"

"Mine and Abigail's."

"I'm so entering that one. What else?"

"In the evening, there's dancing."

"No fireworks?"

"I've heard they used to, but ever since Zane McGavin spoke to the town council and explained the danger to eagles, they gave up fireworks for good."

"How are they a problem for eagles? They don't fly at night."

"They will if they get scared by fireworks. They'll abandon their nests for the season, maybe forever. If babies are in the nest, they die."

Pete gave a low whistle of surprise. "I had no idea."

"I didn't know that, either," Wes said. "Good for Zane. And you said there's dancing?"

"There was last year. The organizers set up a wooden dance floor and a bandstand. The Guzzling Grizzly hired one of their regular country groups to play and likely will again, but this year Nicole and Bryce will perform, too."

"Sounds like fun," Pete said.

"And also like it could go late," Wes added.

"They usually wrap up about eleven or eleven thirty. I won't make it that long, though. I have to be up at three again tomorrow to start baking."

Wes chuckled. "I'll be lucky to make it past sundown."

"Oh?"

"Wes spent the night helping a foal enter the world," Pete said. "He climbed in bed about an hour after you got up this morning. He's running on fumes."

Ingrid leaned around him so she could look at his face. "Should you even be here?"

"I'm not about to miss my first Fourth of July celebration in Eagles Nest. I'll catch up on my sleep later."

"We're almost there," Pete said. "Tell you what. You two climb down and get in line for some breakfast. I'll take the horses over to the trailer."

"Wait, that's not fair. Let me do it since you brought them out here."

"Be sensible, Wes. I've had breakfast and a good night's sleep. Go get yourself some chow and coffee before you fall over. You can buy me a beer later if that would ease your conscience."

"I'll do that. And thanks, bro."

"Any time, Doc. Which reminds me. Dad wanted me to ask if there's any chance you could come out and look at Banjo sometime soon. He's been favoring his right foreleg. But he knows you're busy and—"

"Not too busy for Dad's horse. I'll make time tomorrow."

"Banjo?" Ingrid glanced at Pete. "I'm loving the names of your horses. Why Banjo?"

"The guy that sold him to my dad said the horse was high-strung. But Dad settled him right down."

"I'll bet he did." She'd been a fan of Quinn Sawyer ever since he'd shown up at the bakery in February looking for Roxanne.

Wes and Pete guided their horses in behind where the GG float parked and pulled them to a halt.

"That was fun." Ingrid let go of Wes and grabbed the saddle as she swung her leg over and slid down. "Thank you. I'm glad you suggested it."

"So am I." He dismounted with the ease of a seasoned horseman. "Can I talk you into having breakfast with me as thanks for the use of your shower?"

She hesitated for only a moment. "Sure, that would be great." Now that they weren't pressed together, she could put him firmly back in the brother/neighbor zone.

"Then let's do it." He handed Fudge's reins up to Pete. "Thanks, again, bro. I'm definitely buying you that beer."

"Never mind." Pete grinned down at him. "I'll put it on your tab."

Wes laughed. "Shoulda seen that coming."

"Just kidding. Nice sharing the ride with you, Ingrid."

"Same here, Pete."

"See you in a few." Leading Fudge, he rode toward the collection of horse trailers at the far side of the park.

Wes glanced in the direction of the food tent. "I can smell the bacon from here. Let's make tracks."

"Works for me." She fell into step beside him. "Why did Pete say he'd put this on your tab?"

"When I was a little kid I figured he could finish every chore faster so I constantly begged him to do mine. He'd give in to shut me up, but he said it was going on my tab. I didn't know what he meant until a couple of months went by and I found out I owed him about a million little favors."

"And you did them?"

"Had to. He reminded me of what Dad kept telling us. Real cowboys, and cowgirls, for that matter, honor their debts and keep their promises. I was his slave for weeks."

"Cute story. Is it true?"

"Mostly. I might have exaggerated how many favors, but I—"

"I mean the part about how real cowboys and cowgirls are expected to act. I've heard people refer to a cowboy code but I thought it might be an old-fashioned idea that nobody pays attention to anymore."

"I can't speak for the general population, but my dad strictly abides by it. It's how we were raised. If you owe a debt, you pay it. If you make a promise, you keep it."

I always keep my promises. Mark's blue eyes had glowed with love and sincerity. Then he'd kissed her one more time, climbed in his car, and driven away.

"Man, that food smells great!" Wes glanced over at her. "What are you in the mood for?"

Disoriented, she fumbled her response. "I...I'm thinking scrambled eggs and...some bacon, maybe hash browns. How about you?"

"Everything. I might even grab two plates. By the time we make it through this line, I'll be ravenous." He motioned for her to go ahead of him as they approached the end of it.

"Maybe I'll add some pancakes, too." She was at a celebration, after all. And she wasn't about to let memories of Mark spoil her day.

3

Something was going on with Ingrid. For a second it was like a cloud had passed over the sun and her eyes got very sad.

If someone had asked Wes an hour ago what color they were, he would have drawn a blank. Now he could describe them. He'd never been to the Caribbean, but he'd seen pictures. Her eyes were like the blue-green water there, except for that one moment when they'd looked almost gray.

"Hey, brother of mine!"

He turned as Roxanne came toward him, her mane of dark hair loose around her shoulders. She'd been wearing it that way more often. Might be because she was crazy in love for the guy walking beside her. "Hey, sis! Hey, Michael!" He hugged his sister and shook hands with Michael as they got into line behind him.

Roxanne gave him a light punch on the shoulder. "I see you talked my bestie into riding down here with you."

"It was fun," Ingrid said.

"I'm sure it was. Wes and Fudge were my means of transportation around the ranch until I turned sixteen and got Scooter."

"Is Scooter out at your dad's place, now?"

"No." Roxanne shook her head and glanced over at Wes with a sad smile. "He's in horsy heaven."

"Aw." Ingrid's brow puckered. "Was he old?"

"Only eight," Roxanne said. "Colic got him. Nasty stuff. But losing Scooter was the defining moment for Wes. That's when he committed to becoming a vet, so something good came out of Scooter's passing."

Wes rolled his eyes. "You make it sound so dramatic."

"It was dramatic! There you were, tears streaming down your face, and you—"

"Tears were *not* streaming down my face."

Roxanne lifted her chin. "Were so."

"It was sweat." His cheeks warmed. Little sisters. Couldn't keep their mouths shut.

"Don't be embarrassed," Ingrid said. "There's nothing unmanly about crying. It shows you're compassionate."

"Um, thanks." He was so done with this discussion. He glanced at his sister. "I don't have to ask what you're getting for breakfast."

"We all know the answer to that one." Michael slid a hand around her waist. "I think you love pancakes more than you do me."

"Not true." She laughed. "But they're super important today. We need to load up on carbs if we're gonna win the three-legged race."

"Who says you're gonna win?" Wes looked over at Ingrid. "I think we can take 'em, don't you?" Bold move to assume she'd agree to be his partner. Stupid move if she declined.

She grinned. "Depends on whether you can stay awake long enough to cross the finish line."

Awesome. Strategy worked. "Give me enough caffeine and sugar and I'll be a racing fool." Then tie him to Ingrid and they might set a world's record. He'd never run a three-legged race before, but how hard could it be?

Bryce and Nicole walked up and got in line behind Michael.

"Sure enjoyed the music this morning," Wes said.

"Thanks." Bryce tipped his hat to Ingrid. "How's my favorite barista?"

"Great. You two sounded wonderful this morning. Is it hard playing while the float's moving?"

"It's tricky." Nicole pulled a hair tie out of her pocket and tied back her red curls. "I hadn't figured out how to keep my balance when we did the Memorial Day one but I was better this time. Speaking of balance, are either of you doing the three-legged race?"

"Yep," Ingrid said. "Wes and I are teaming up."

"Bryce talked me into it, too. He said it's fun, but I've never done it before so I'm a little leery."

"I've never done it, either," Wes said, "but it seems pretty straightforward."

Ingrid blinked. "You've never done it?"

"No, but I'm a decent runner. I was the tight end on my high school football team."

"It's not the same." She gave him a quick smile. "But you'll find that out in about an hour."

Roxanne peered around his shoulder. "You've never run a three-legged race? How did you miss out, big brother? I've done it a bunch of times."

"I'll bet that's when you went to summer camp."

"Probably, now that you say that. I went because they had crafts, but we had other stuff."

"I ran my first one last Fourth of July," Michael said. "It wasn't pretty. But at least I know what I'm up against. And I have to warn the newbies—the McGavins have a lock on this event."

"That's the truth," Bryce said. "We dominated in the twelve-and-under category when we were kids, and we're doing the same now that we're in the big group."

"And by *big group*," Michael said, "he means it's everybody else, all ages from twelve on up."

Wes blinked. "Seniors, too?"

"Our seniors would be insulted if we separated them out." Bryce grinned. "You should see Ellie Mae out there. She and Cody won it one year, despite the fact she's a foot shorter and sixty years older than he is. They—" He paused as Nicole handed him a plate. "Tell you more after we get some food."

After loading their plates, they gathered at a long picnic table and Wes soaked up info as the McGavins reminisced about past events. Trevor, Bryce's twin, joined them with his girlfriend, Olivia. Then the newlyweds, Cody and Faith, arrived with their food.

Wes scooted closer to Ingrid to make room and Faith ended up next to him. She promptly announced that she was doing the three-legged race with Cody even if she was four months pregnant. "Because of our trip last summer, we missed all this, so I want to do everything."

Ellie Mae came up behind them and laid one hand on Cody's shoulder and the other on Faith's. "But you stole my favorite race partner."

Faith glanced up at her and smiled. "I'm sorry, ma'am. But rank has its privileges."

"I know that, honey. I just came over to see if you and Cody have said anything about the fundraiser. This is a great time to spread the word."

"Oh! I plumb forgot."

Trevor nudged back his hat. "What fundraiser?"

"It started out as a betting pool," Cody said. "Faith and I were having sundaes in Pills and Pop when Ellie Mae mentioned that folks were betting on whether we'd have a boy or a girl."

"I heard that," Michael said. "I thought it was a joke."

"It was happening," Cody said. "So we decided to take charge of it, make it a public thing. Ellie Mae's now holding all the bets and—"

"That makes me a bookie." She sounded pleased about it.

Trevor scrubbed a hand over his face. "This is sounding stranger by the minute."

"We thought so, too," Faith said. "That's why we put a charitable twist on it. The baby's due the middle of December, so twenty-five percent of the proceeds will go toward holiday baskets for needy families."

Michael nodded. "Good plan. I like it."

"It's a great idea." Wes took his wallet out of his back pocket. "And I've got twenty bucks that says Faith is having a girl."

"I'll put my money on a baby boy." Ingrid fished in her pocket. "Boys run in the McGavin family."

"But the law of averages says this one will be a girl." Olivia slapped down a twenty. "I'm betting that Kendra gets a granddaughter. She would love that so much."

The noise level rose as the group called out their bets and held out money.

"Slow down, everybody." Ellie Mae produced a folded sheet of paper and a stub of a pencil. "I have to record all this."

"I'll help." Wes glanced up at her. "If you collect the money, I'll keep track of the bets."

"Thank you, Wes." Ellie Mae smiled at him and handed over her paper and pencil. "We need to get cracking, though. The little kids' race just started and we're up next."

"We'll work fast." Wes quickly wrote down the info as she called it out.

After placing their bets, people cleared their empty plates and cups and left for the race. Eventually Wes and Ellie Mae were the only ones at the table. Ingrid had gathered up their trash and was taking it to the recycling bin.

She returned and glanced at Wes. "We'd better get over there and put our names in, too."

"Yes, you should," Ellie Mae said. "Thanks for the help, Wes." She tucked everything into a pouch that hung from her neck. "Let's move." She started off at a brisk pace.

Wes and Ingrid had to hustle to keep up with her.

"Is it just Wes or Wesley?" Ellie Mae didn't break stride or even look at him.

"Wesley's the long version but I like the short one better. It's what my friends call me."

"Understood. Oh, there's my race partner." She waved at a gray-haired man on the far side of the field. "He's got it into his head that racing together means I want to get frisky. But he's not my type. See you!" She hurried off.

Wes looked at Ingrid. "Ready to do this thing?"

Her eyes were that blue-green happy color. "Yes, I am."

"Thanks for agreeing to be my partner. I'll give it all I've got."

"I have no doubt. That's one of the things I like about you, Wes."

Well, now. That sounded promising.

4

As the experienced racer, Ingrid took the lead in getting them registered and grabbing one of the Velcro straps heaped in a bin on the registration table. She suggested moving off to the side so they could strap up and take a few practice runs.

She faced him, holding the strap. "Are you right or left-handed?"

"Right."

"That helps. I'm left-handed. You should be on my right, which puts our two non-dominant legs together."

"So you'll lead with your left foot and I'll lead with my right?"

"That's the idea. It worked with Abigail and me last year, but then again, we're close to the same height. You and I aren't, so our bodies don't match up very well."

Wes ducked his head, but she still heard his soft chuckle.

"Hey."

"Couldn't help it." He glanced up and almost succeeded in looking contrite. "You sounded so serious when you said that."

She gave him a mock glare. "This is serious business, buster."

"I can see that."

And she intended to keep their focus on the task at hand. "Line up next to me so I can wrap this thing around our ankles."

"Y'all need help gettin' hitched?"

She looked over and there was Badger, out of uniform and back in his cowboy duds. He and his sweetheart Hayley walked toward them holding hands.

"Badger's appointed himself the official hitcher-upper." Hayley tucked her blonde hair behind her ears.

"Because it needs doin'," Badger said. "Y'all don't have the right angle to create the perfect connection. Let me have y'all's strap."

"Yeah, okay." She got such a kick out of Badger. And it would be easier for him to tighten the strap.

He took the strap and crouched down in front of them. "Get closer. Put your arms around each other."

Uh-oh. She hadn't anticipated this part. But she wasn't going to back out now. She aligned herself with Wes and slid her arm around his waist. Yep, she'd been right. Not an ounce of fat on the guy. Curiosity got the better of her. "Do you work out?"

"Yeah." He chuckled. "I work out of my truck."

She gave him a look. "I meant in a gym."

"There's a gym in Eagles Nest?"

"No, but—"

"There you go." Badger engaged the Velcro strip and snugged her ankle up against Wes's. "You're a team, now. My blessings on y'all. Have a safe and mutually satisfyin' race."

"Thanks, Badger." Ingrid tested the connection and it was solid. "What about you and Hayley? Aren't you going to race?"

"Oh, we will. Once I finish helpin' folks hitch up, Ryker's promised to do the honors for us."

"Then you'd better go find him." Ingrid checked the time on her phone. "The race is supposed to start in five minutes."

"She's right. We should go," Hayley said. "We need to give you and Wes a couple of minutes to practice."

"Thanks." Ingrid glanced up at the man tethered to her ankle. "We need to start off at the same time. Let's do a countdown."

"Okay, you do the counting."

She nodded. "On three, step forward with your dominant leg and I'll do the same. One…two…*three.*" She took a step and immediately lost her balance because he'd taken a much bigger step.

"Whoops." He grabbed her arm and edged back so their outside feet were parallel. "Took too big a stride."

"Yeah, you'll have to shorten it. Let's bring our inside legs up even with…whoa!" She grabbed onto him again as he moved before she was ready. She hopped on her free foot until she had both feet on the ground.

"I thought you meant to do it right then."

"No, I—here's an idea. Let's pretend like we're dancing and count it out as we go."

"Sounds good. You do the counting."

"All right. When I say *one*, we both move our outside legs. When I say *two* we both move our inside legs."

"Got it."

"Then let's—"

"Attention big group! Gather at the starting line!" The voice was male and bristling with authority.

Wes glanced up. "Was that *Ryker*?"

"Oh, yeah. That's his military command voice."

"Ha! Clearly Ryker don't need no stinkin' bullhorn."

Ingrid laughed. "No, he does not. Okay, our first task is to get to the starting line, so I'll count in reverse from three to one so we can walk ourselves over there. When I say *one*, we'll start off with the *one-two, one-two* cadence."

"I just have something to say."

"Say it quick."

"There's an excellent chance we'll fall, so if you feel yourself going down, land on me."

She was so not going to picture that scenario. "We won't fall. Here we go. *Three, two, one-two, one-two, one-two.*" Their herky-jerky progress made her laugh and she bobbled the count.

Wes picked it up. "*One-two, one-two, one-two.* And we're here!" He sent her a grin of triumph.

They joined the linked-up racers positioned side-by-side across a wide swath of field. She and Wes were second from the left. Zane and Mandy McGavin were on the end, both wearing Raptors Rise t-shirts. Mandy's mom, Jo, stood nearby with the starting whistle around her neck.

"Morning, Ingrid." Zane tipped his hat in her direction.

"Hi, Zane. Hi, Mandy. Jo, you're not racing?"

Jo sighed. "Dropped a jar of pickles on my toe the other day and broke it."

"Ouch! Sorry."

"That's okay. Somebody needs to be the official starter. We always have trouble finding—"

"Aw, geez." From down the line on Ingrid's right, Trevor let out a groan. "Mom, what are you wearing? Oh, no. Quinn's wearing them, too."

Using Wes for support, Ingrid leaned forward. Kendra and Quinn's white canvas shoes glowed like searchlights in a row of brown boots.

"They're running shoes," Kendra said. "As if you didn't know. This is a race, isn't it?"

"A race where everyone wears boots," Trevor said. "Because we're in Montana and it's traditional to race in boots. Ryker, did you see this travesty?"

"I did." Ryker's voice boomed from the far end of the line. "And I expressed my opinion."

Quinn laughed. "And we respectfully declined to listen. We're starting a new trend."

"Kendra must be shaking things up," Wes said in an undertone. "I've never seen my dad wear shoes like that."

"I think they're kind of cute, Wes." Zane's voice was loud enough to carry. "I mean, when you get to be a certain age, you—"

"Make fun all you want, son," Kendra called out. "You'll end up eating our dust."

"But they're dorky," Cody said. "Love you, Mom. Becoming fond of you, too, Quinn. But those shoes don't improve your look. Just sayin'."

"That's fine with us." Kendra gazed up at Quinn. "Just so it improves our racing, right?"

"Right."

"Ryker?" Jo called across the field. "Are we good to go?"

"Let 'er rip, Aunt Jo!"

Ingrid glanced at Wes and mouthed *one-two, one-two*.

He nodded.

The shrill blast from Jo's whistle set off a deafening stampede. Ingrid counted as loud as she could and Wes must have heard her because they stayed in step. For a while. Until they didn't.

She stumbled and Wes lifted her off her feet as they both started to fall. He hit the ground with a thud and held onto her so she couldn't avoid landing smack-dab on top of him. His loud *oof* was followed by tortured gasping for air. Great. She'd knocked the wind out of him.

Rolling away to take the weight off his chest, she sat up, sucked in a few lungsful of air and reached for the Velcro strap.

"No." His voice was strangled.

"Yes." She pulled off the strap and took another deep breath. "We did very well for the first time running together. There's no shame in calling it at this point. We made it halfway."

"Not good enough." He sat up, looked around for his hat and plucked it off the ground. "We need to finish."

"At the pace we were going, it will take us until tomorrow."

"You exaggerate."

"A little, but people are already crossing the finish line." She held the strap out of reach. "It's okay, Wes. We can plan for next summer's race and get in some practice between now and then."

"Yeah?" His dark eyes regained their sparkle. "You'd be willing to do that?"

Alarms rang in her head, but she couldn't very well take it back. "Sure, why not?"

"Might be difficult once it snows."

"We can race up and down the hall."

That made him laugh. "There's an image."

"Isn't it, though?" She was adding fuel to the fire, but she couldn't seem to keep her mouth shut.

"Alrighty, then. Next year we'll kick butt." He dusted off his hat, settled it on his head and got to his feet. "But I still want to finish this race." He held out his hand.

"You're not getting the strap." She rolled it into a tight cylinder and stuck it in the only place she could think of where it would stay put—down the front of her blouse, tucked into her bra.

"You're right. I'm too much of a gentleman. But at least let me help you up."

"Okay." She put her hand in his.

He pulled her to her feet. "We're finishing the race." He scooped her into his arms.

"Hey! Carrying me there doesn't count!" And being in his arms was doing dangerous things to her pulse.

"It should count double." He started off at a fast walk that turned into a jog.

"Stop! This is crazy!"

He gulped for air. "Better'n dragging across...the finish line...with our tail...between our legs."

"Good Lord. You're certifiable." And she was enjoying this way too much. He'd promised her he'd give it all he had and he was true to his word.

Someone must have noticed them coming across the empty field, because as they approached, all the racers lined up and began clapping and cheering. Phone cameras came out. Winning the race would have been gratifying, but this was way more memorable.

He crossed the finish line and continued to hold her as he gasped for breath. "We did it."

"You did it." She patted his sweat-dampened cheek. "Good job. Now put me down, please." She needed some space to regain her equilibrium.

He set her carefully on her feet as everyone shoved water bottles and towels at them. She took the water but backed away to let them fuss over Wes.

Abigail came over with Delilah trotting at her heels and Ingrid crouched down to love on the border collie. "Where have you been, girl?"

"We put her in the truck during the race," Abigail said. "She would have loved running with us, but there were a million ways that could have gone bad."

"Well, she's here, now." Ingrid buried her fingers in Delilah's thick ruff and gave her a kiss on the nose.

Delilah's tail wagged a mile a minute. She gave Ingrid a tiny swipe on the nose in return.

"And so happy to be with her peeps." Abigail glanced over at the group clustered around Wes. "I'll bet that move was a first. We should ask someone who's lived here longer." She raised her voice. "Kendra, has anybody ever carried their racing partner across the finish line?"

"I don't think so." She walked toward them, still wearing her running shoes. Quinn was with the crowd gathered around his son. "I missed one race when I had the flu, but I would have heard about it if anybody had done that." She leaned down to stroke Delilah. "Hey, pup. Good to see you."

"Wes broke the rules of the game, of course," Ingrid said.

"He did, but what a swashbuckling move." Kendra chuckled. "He's clearly his father's son. Gallant gestures seem to be a Sawyer specialty."

"I'm getting that." She stood and glanced over at Wes, the hero of the hour even though they'd come in dead last.

He looked in her direction, smiled and lifted his water bottle in a silent toast. She lifted hers in return, but the telltale flutter in her stomach made her uneasy. She'd have to be clear that they were just keeping it friendly.

5

Wes hadn't factored in the dynamic now that his dad was in a relationship with Kendra. Even though they weren't married, weren't even living together, they'd become the de facto heads of an extended family. And the Eagles Nest Fourth of July celebration was all about family.

Everybody seemed to assume that Ingrid was with Wes for the day. He was fine with that and she made no move to excuse herself, so evidently she was okay with the arrangement, too. When someone wanted a group photo, she seemed happy to be in the picture.

Hanging out with Ingrid while surrounded by friends and family made for a fun-filled, no-pressure situation. It wasn't a date, although carrying her across the finish line had shifted the dynamic. He was a lot more aware of her than he had been the past month. Being with her added spice to every activity, even though the atmosphere was as wholesome as a church picnic.

The pie-eating contest contributed to that downhome vibe. Wes entered as he'd promised Ingrid he would. The pies were delicious, but afterward he kept visualizing Ingrid up to her elbows in flour, her cheeks flushed, as she made the crusts and spooned in the filling.

Sexy image, at least to him. He hadn't thought of her that way before. It was part of the reason that being with her gave him a buzz and contributed to his efforts as he fought to stay awake. He maintained his energy level until dinnertime, when he made the mistake of having a beer with his meal. He'd bought a beer for Pete as promised and had managed to add in dinner. He'd talked Ingrid into letting him treat her, too.

The McGavin/Sawyer contingent had snagged a couple of large tables near the bandstand and the music was toe-tapping wonderful. Wes enjoyed the heck out of the food, the tunes and his beer until he made it to the bottom of his mug. Then exhaustion hit him between the eyes.

"Hey, little brother." Pete reached across the table and squeezed his arm. "I think you're done."

He took a deep breath and straightened. "I don't want to be done. I'm having too much fun."

Ingrid leaned closer and peered into his face. "You can barely keep your eyes open, buster."

"I just need to move, that's all." He flattened his hands on the table and pushed himself up before climbing over the attached bench seat. "Would you like to dance?"

She gave him a worried look. "Wes, I don't think that's a good—"

"The band is terrific. Don't you think it's terrific? Come on. It's a two-step. Let's grab our chance before it's finished. I love me a good two-step. That'll get my blood flowing again." He held out his hand.

She glanced at it with a small frown. "Okay. One dance." She put her hand in his. "Or half a dance, anyway."

"Thanks." She was probably tired, too. But getting on their feet would shake off the sleepiness. Touching her was a bonus. He got a reviving jolt of sensation when he clasped her hand and helped her out of her seat. Then he led her up the steps to the dance platform.

Marshalling his forces, he slipped an arm around her waist and swung her neatly into the kaleidoscope of dancers already on the floor. A couple was right on their heels, but he picked up the pace and avoided a collision.

"Fancy meeting you here." His dad twirled Kendra under his arm. They'd ditched the running shoes in favor of boots. "Aren't you ready to pack it in, son?"

"Not yet." He executed a similar move with Ingrid. "What happened to the running shoes?"

"They served their purpose," Kendra said.

"Did you guys win? I'm embarrassed to admit I didn't get that info."

"We won," his dad said, "and you can bet folks will be wearing them next year. But you gotta have boots for dancing." He whirled Kendra in one direction and back in the other.

"Especially fancy dancing." Ingrid looked up at Wes. "Can you do that?"

"Only on Wednesdays."

"But it's—"

"So it is." He navigated the double whirl. "The big guy taught me everything he knows."

His dad laughed. "Not quite."

"What? You've been holding out on me?"

"Never. But some things a man has to learn for himself." He smiled at Kendra. "Agreed?"

"Couldn't have said it better."

"Hey, Wes." His dad did the double twirl thing again. "If you leave before I do, I—"

"Banjo. Pete told me. Afternoon?"

"That works."

"I'll text you."

"Do that. In case I'm over at Wild Creek." The music stopped and he glanced down at Kendra. "Ready to relax with a beer?"

"You know it." She turned to Wes and Ingrid. "Want to join us?"

"Thanks, but no thanks," Wes said, "One more beer and I'll have to be carried home."

After his dad and Kendra walked away, their arms around each other's waists, Ingrid lowered her voice. "They're so cute together."

"Yep." The band launched into a slow tune and Ingrid was right there, so he pulled her into his arms and moved gently with the music. "I always thought my dad had created the perfect life for himself. He seemed completely satisfied with it. But when I see him with Kendra...he's so much more vibrant now."

"She is, too. She had a fabulous setup, but Quinn turned out to be the part she didn't know she was missing." She blinked. "Wait. I said we'd only do one dance. Now we're—"

"It's a cool-down dance." He linked his hands behind her back and gazed into her Caribbean blue eyes. "The other one was like a canter over the meadow. This is like a slow walk back to the barn."

"A canter over the meadow." Her expression softened. "That sounds nice."

"It is. We should do it sometime." His hips brushed hers, but the contact was subtle, just enough to keep his buzz going. Her blonde ponytail swayed gently in time with the music.

"I don't have a horse."

"I do. And we could borrow Clifford or Banjo."

"Does your dad have a meadow?"

"A small one. Kendra has way more property. Cantering over her meadows would be a lot more fun."

"Have you ever done that?"

"Too busy. Today was the first time I've been on Fudge since I got here."

"But you obviously love riding."

"Sure do. Nothing like seeing the world from the back of a horse." He gazed at her. "Want to go riding with me?"

She didn't respond right away. A small line appeared between her brows, too. Maybe they weren't on the same page.

"All right."

Or maybe they were. "When?"

"I have Sundays off unless Abigail and I have to do some emergency pie baking."

He smiled. "I'm picturing disaster sirens blaring as you grab your rolling pins and speed-roll those crusts."

"It sometimes feels that way. If the Guzzling Grizzly runs out on Saturday night, they'll request additional inventory for their Sunday crowd. If our stash is low, we sometimes bake on Sunday morning. Abigail hates disappointing her best customer."

"Makes sense. I admire that kind of dedication."

"Me, too. I can't believe you're still upright after getting so little sleep, though."

"It's a mind game. I'm visualizing being well-rested and able to last another couple of hours out here."

"How's that working for you?"

"Just great, as long as we keep dancing."

"I hate to tell you, but the song's over."

"It is?" He paused. Silence. "Huh. That's okay. They'll—"

"We're taking a short break folks," the lead singer said. "Be back in a few."

"Hm." He was reluctant to let go of her. Losing that contact might make him crash. "Maybe I should get some coffee."

Ingrid smiled. "And maybe you should just give up and go home."

"But I—"

"I should, too. I've been up since three and I'll be up at three again tomorrow. Going home now would be a smart move."

"You're sure?"

"Yep. It's been a fun day but a long one. I'm going to say my goodbyes and mosey on back."

"Then how about I walk you home?"

"Okay."

After making the rounds to bid everyone goodbye, he walked beside her out to the street. "Sure is nice out."

"I like this time of evening when there's still a tinge of pink in the sky. The air's the perfect temperature."

"And nobody's out here. We can stroll down the middle of the street if we want."

"Then let's." She walked along one side of the yellow line.

He took the other side, leaving the space of the stripe between them. He had the strongest urge to reach for her hand. But if he did that, and she pulled away, that would be a sucky ending to a nearly perfect day. Why risk it?

The street lamps flickered on and she let out a happy little sigh. "I love those lamps. I love this town. I'm so glad I moved here."

"Why did you?"

"I was in culinary school over at U of M and decided to take a drive. Stopped in at Pie in the Sky and fell in love with Abigail's setup. Owning a bakery like hers was my dream, so when she asked if I wanted a job, I took it."

"What about school?"

"I figured I'd learn as much, maybe more, working for Abigail, plus I'd get paid for it. I also fell in love with Eagles Nest."

"Do you still want to open your own bakery?"

"That goal's changed some. This town's not big enough for two bakeries. But I've paid attention to what Michael did over at the GG, working his way up from employee to co-owner."

"Would Abigail consider something similar and make you a partner?"

"She might. I haven't mentioned it to her, but she keeps giving me more responsibility. For now, I'm happy with things as they are."

"I considered looking for a partner when I decided to go the mobile vet route. But I wasn't positive that Eagles Nest could support one vet, let alone two."

"What do you think, now?"

He laughed. "I think Kendra's beating the bushes to find me jobs. I want to believe all those folks really need dental checks on their horses, but I suspect a few have made appointments as a favor to Kendra."

"Then you'll have to let things settle out before you know what your true income will be."

"Exactly. Which is another reason to take every appointment that comes my way, in case I end up with some dry spells."

"Just don't run yourself ragged."

"Ah, I won't. I'm healthy as a..." He paused. "I never thought about it before, but that expression makes no sense. Horses are more delicate than most people realize."

"Like Scooter."

"Um, yeah, like Scooter. Anyway, speaking of appointments, I have one for nine in the morning. I happened to see our landlady today, so I asked about the shower. She won't be able to get a plumber to look at it until tomorrow afternoon. Could I—"

"Of course."

"I'll bring my own soap and shampoo this time. That was lame of me."

"No problem. You were in a hurry."

"I tried to be neat, though."

"I'm sure you did." She smiled. "Hey, we're here already."

"Let me get the door." He fished out his key.

"It feels like it's been such a long time since the parade."

"Probably because we did a lot, today." He opened the door and motioned her inside. An overhead fixture in the entry and another in the upstairs hall lit the stairs as she began the climb, her footsteps on the wooden steps echoing in the silence.

He supposed they'd been alone in this building lots of times, but it hadn't registered the way it did tonight. Abigail had held onto the front apartment even though she, Luke and Delilah spent most of their time at his house adjacent to Wild Creek Ranch. Every so often they spent the night here, and he hadn't kept track of whether there was a routine to it.

For now, it was just Ingrid and him. And the poster on her wall. *A woman needs a man like a fish needs a bicycle.* He'd laughed at it this morning. After spending a wonderful day with her, he'd lost his sense of humor concerning that piece of art. He followed her up the stairs.

She waited for him at the top as he mounted the last couple of steps. "Thank you for inviting me to ride down to the park with you today." Her mouth tilted in a soft smile. "I had a really good time."

"So did I." He nudged back his hat and cleared his throat. "I just have to ask. What's that poster on your wall all about?"

Her smile faded.

Way to ruin the mood, idiot. "Never mind. Shouldn't have asked. It's none of my business."

"I wouldn't say that." She took a breath. "But if you don't mind, I'd rather not talk about it tonight."

"You don't have to talk about it, ever."

"I wondered if Roxanne might have—"

"No."

She nodded. "I should have known she wouldn't. She's a good friend."

Terrific. He'd just turned a sweet moment into an awkward one. "I should let you go, then. I'll...see you around." He started to turn away.

"Wait."

He glanced at her. Those gorgeous blue eyes had lost their sparkle, damn it. "Listen, I'm sorry I mentioned the poster. It's just that I didn't remember seeing it the first time I was in your apartment."

"I put it up three weeks ago. It's...a long story, one better told another time." She stepped closer. "Thank you for a great day." Without warning, she lifted to her toes and gave him a quick kiss on the mouth. Then she spun around and hurried down the hallway. Her door closed behind her with a soft click.

He stood where he was for a while, lips tingling from her drive-by kiss. What the hell did *that* mean?

6

Ingrid closed her door and leaned against it. An impulsive thank-you kiss had not been smart. Yes, she'd had a lovely day and she was grateful for that. It didn't justify kissing him.

The festivities had interrupted or at least grayed-out the endless loop of regrets and heartache she'd been slogging through ever since flying home from Boston. That might have happened without Wes being such a big part of the day, but maybe not.

Was she attracted to him? Well, yeah. What woman wouldn't be? But she could squash that, no problem. Her battered heart couldn't take any more blows right now. And she certainly didn't want to get involved with her best friend's brother.

She'd made a mistake by kissing him, but not a huge one. First chance she had, she'd give him a quick overview of her situation so he'd get it.

* * *

Until three weeks ago, Ingrid had been a champion sleeper. The disastrous trip to Boston had changed that and she'd been plagued with restless nights and bad dreams. Theoretically a whole day spent outdoors with plenty of exercise should have allowed her to sleep like a baby.

Instead she tossed and turned. When she did sleep, conflicting images of Wes and Mark filled her dreams, batting her emotions back and forth like a tennis ball.

Groaning, she turned the pillow to the cool side, but that didn't help. She climbed out of bed at three with a sigh of relief. Thank God for this job. It was her saving grace.

Since the Boston trip, kneading dough, and occasionally pounding the heck out of it, had become therapy. Pulling fragrant loaves and pastries out of the oven lifted her spirits, as did mixing her favorite coffee drinks. She couldn't wait to get down there.

Her morning shower was a little weird, though, since Wes had been the last one to use it. She liked to leave the soap propped on its narrow side so it drained better. He'd left it flat. He'd switched the position of the shampoo and conditioner bottles, too.

In general, though, he'd been extremely neat considering how rushed he'd been. He'd respected her space. And he'd be back again this morning. That thought was a little unsettling, especially after the dreams she'd had.

She tidied up more than usual before leaving the apartment. Then she crept softly along the hall and down the stairs so her footsteps wouldn't disturb him. Until now she'd been oblivious to the noise she made leaving her place. A sleeping Wes hadn't been on her radar.

He was certainly on her radar now. Good thing she was heading down to the bakery. Work would jolt her away from her unwelcome thoughts regarding her neighbor.

Luke dropped Abigail off as Ingrid unlocked the bakery's front door. She waved at him and he flashed his headlights before pulling away from the curb.

"You were smart, going home when you did." Abigail followed her inside and locked up after them. "Luke and I stayed too late and I'm going to pay for it today." She flipped on the lights.

"Then how about if I crank up the espresso machine and make us each a Firecracker?"

"I'd be all over that. While you make it, I'll prep for the first round."

"Sounds like a plan." Ingrid adored the shiny espresso machine. Specialty coffee paired beautifully with her first love—baked goods. Abigail used to serve only basic brewed coffee. Thanks to a suggestion from Luke, Pie in the Sky now offered a wide range of coffee drinks, with a signature brew for each holiday. Ingrid's former barista experience had come in handy.

The Firecracker wasn't for the faint of heart, though. Ingrid had created it partly for herself, to offset her recent insomnia. It included three shots of espresso laced with a cinnamon flavoring that tasted like red-hots. She'd located a supply of flag-themed mugs for serving the foamy concoction. Customers who drank it swore they saw stars.

When she brought two mugs over to one of the bistro tables, Abigail was already there.

At each place, she'd set a cheese Danish on a plate along with a neatly folded napkin. "I figured if we were going to do this we might as well do it right."

"I'll go along with that." She took her seat and picked up her mug. "To a power breakfast."

Abigail laughed. "A caffeine and sugar high that should carry us for at least...an hour?"

"Maybe longer. The cheese counts as protein, right?"

"Absolutely." Abigail took a mouthful of coffee and swallowed. Then she gasped and waved her hand in front of her face. "Damn, that's potent."

"That's the idea. There's a reason we have a warning posted." Ingrid approached her drink with caution. She'd invented it and she also respected the heck out of it. Proceeding one tiny sip at a time, she allowed the coffee to sweep the cobwebs from her brain. "Ah, that's better."

"Bad night again?"

"Not great."

"Damn. I'm sorry." Abigail's jaw tightened. Despite her short curly hair and soft features, she was intimidating when she was angry. "Mark's lucky he's so far away."

"He's not worth thinking about." She told herself that every day. So far the concept hadn't taken hold.

"True, but I want to see him suffer. I want to see him squirm and beg for mercy."

"Karma will get him, right?"

"I suppose, but how will we know? I want to be right there when that cheating bastard gets what's coming to him."

"Thank you for that." Ingrid reached across the table and squeezed her arm. "Especially when you've never met him."

"I've never met him, but I've met his kind—the face of an angel and a black hole where his heart should be." She shuddered.

"I'm well rid of him." Something else she told herself on a regular basis. Her head knew it but her heart hadn't gotten the message yet.

"You absolutely are, but that doesn't make me any less furious." She polished off her coffee and brushed the cheese Danish crumbs from her fingers. "Ready?"

"Let's do it."

Ingrid lost herself in her work, one of the many benefits of what had turned out to be the perfect job. She and Abigail had teamwork down to an art. Surrounded by the sparkling kitchen surfaces and the aroma of bread, pastries and pies baking, Ingrid gave thanks for the road trip that had brought her to Eagles nest and Pie in the Sky. She belonged here.

The other two employees, Yolanda and Doug, arrived a little before six. They sailed in just ahead of eager customers who'd begun filling the diagonal parking spaces in front.

Ingrid met Doug over by the espresso machine. He loved it as much as she did and had become a talented barista in only a few months. Good thing, because early mornings they were usually swamped with coffee orders.

Before Ingrid could blink, another two hours had flown by and customer traffic had tapered off. She had a moment to catch her breath and make herself another cup of coffee, a regular latte this time instead of a Firecracker.

She'd nearly finished her coffee when Kendra came in and hurried over to the bistro table where she was sitting. "Oh, good. I caught you when it's slow."

Ingrid left her chair. "Want some coffee? I can get—"

"Thanks, but I have a bunch of errands to run this morning and I told Quinn I'd bring him lunch. Taking yesterday off put him behind on his latest scratchboard project."

"Is it another big one?"

"Yep. Somebody bought the one hanging in the GG and he didn't have anything to put in its place. Anyway, I came in to ask if I can have some of your pictures from yesterday. I saw you with your phone out, especially during the pie-eating contest."

"I did. What are you doing with them?"

"I'm gathering them to post on the town's website. I'll get permission from everyone, first, but I thought it would be a fun way to share memories of the day."

"People will love that." Ingrid called over to Abigail in the kitchen. "Do you have your phone? Kendra needs some pictures."

"It's in the office. Let me get it."

Ingrid stood and walked behind the counter. "I have a great one of Wes with his face covered in red cherry juice after he won the pie-eating contest. You said you'd check with people before using anything, right?"

"Right. I'll just email them the picture and they can email me back with permission."

Ingrid glanced at her. "You have everybody's email?"

"Just about. A couple of years ago the Whine and Cheese Club made it our project to gather them up. The directory is on the password protected part of the town website."

"That's awesome." She looked for her phone in its usual spot tucked under the counter but it wasn't there. "You know what? I left my phone in my apartment."

"You can text them to me later."

"When are you posting them on the website?"

"Roxanne and Quinn are coming over this afternoon to help me curate them and I want to make sure I—"

"Let me run up and get it. Then it's done and I know I won't forget." She grabbed her keys and left. The shot of Wes was hysterical. It needed to be on the website, assuming he was okay with it.

She'd climbed the stairs and started down the hall when Wes barreled out of her apartment...wearing only a towel.

He skidded to a stop and gulped. "Oh, hey. I...uh...running late...I'll just...get...out of your way." Holding the towel around his hips with one hand and clutching his shampoo and soap with the other, he walked quickly past her trailing the scent of fresh pine.

Like a flower pivoting toward the sun, she slowly turned and watched him stride the rest of the way down the hall, step into his apartment and nudge the door shut with his hip.

Lordy. She dragged in air and pressed a hand to her chest. That image was permanently burned into her retina, now. When she closed her eyes, there he was in all his glory, an everlasting hologram—wet hair in wild disarray, dark stubble giving him a rakish look.

She'd never seen those broad shoulders and powerful arms when they weren't covered by a shirt. Or his shapely pecs. The drops of moisture clinging to his chest hair had quivered with each breath. He'd been breathing fast, too, working those six-pack abs. And then she'd been shown the flip side—his muscular back and his tight buns shifting beneath the towel, thighs and calves flexing as he beat a retreat.

She made her way to her apartment in a daze. The aroma of his piney soap and shampoo greeted her. She followed the scent to her bathroom where it was strongest. The fog was beginning to clear from the mirror but the shower stall was still beaded with water. Taking a deep breath, she left the bathroom and located her phone.

By the time she returned to the bakery, she was breathing normally. But the potent image of Wes lingered. How the hell was she supposed to deal with that?

7

Wes finished with his last client and texted his dad in the late afternoon. His dad was over at Kendra's but said he'd come home immediately for the consultation on Banjo's foreleg.

The *gentleman's ranch* as his dad called it, was down a winding dirt road. Wes hadn't been on the road for more than a week and it had been graded since he last drove it.

The ranch house looked more lived in, too. The front porch had four rockers on it and flowers bloomed in newly created beds on either side of the porch steps.

A path around to the rear of the property had been weeded and raked. His dad had a studio back there and had made good use of it since moving to Eagles Nest. He devoted several hours every morning to his art.

Wes parked next to the house and was climbing the porch steps when his dad rode in on Fudge. Wes came back down the steps. "Place looks great!"

"Thanks. Stole your horse." He reined in the glossy bay and swung down from the saddle.

"I'm glad you did. Thanks for giving him some exercise." He walked over and hugged his dad. The guy looked ten years younger. Clearly he'd made the right decision in selling the Lazy S so he could spend time with Kendra and devote himself to his art.

"You'll get back to riding once you settle into a routine. In the meantime, Pete and I will see that Fudge doesn't get barn sour."

"Thanks, Dad. Matter of fact, I asked Ingrid if she'd like to go riding and she's game. We might even go this Sunday."

"Glad to hear it." His father started toward the barn with Fudge, and Wes fell into step beside him. "She can ride Banjo unless he's not up to it."

"Thanks. If not Banjo, maybe Pete would loan me Clifford."

"Or ask Kendra for a horse. I assume you'd ride on her property."

"That was my thought. Is it strange, not being surrounded by acres of your own?"

"Different, that's for sure."

He glanced at his dad. "Claustrophobic?"

"I wouldn't say that, exactly. But I've been in contact with the folks who have the land to the west of me."

"See, I knew it. You're a land baron. Always have been."

"It's a steal, Wes. Unimproved, not so much as a shack on it. They live back East somewhere. Bought it as an investment twenty years ago. I've made an offer. I think they'll take it."

Wes laughed. "I'm not the least bit surprised that you're adding to your holdings down here. Whatcha going to do with it?"

"Nothing for now. I just...like having it there."

"Did you tell Kendra about this potential land purchase?"

"She knows my every move, son. Other than a romantic surprise now and then, I don't keep anything from her."

"That's good. That's real good."

"It is. I can tell her anything. She never flinches."

"Whereas your kids, on the other hand..."

"Aw, hell, you're entitled to flinch. You've put up with me all these years."

"And you've put up with us. I'm sure we've given you a lot of reasons to flinch."

"Not as much as you might think." He ground-tied Fudge. "Do you have another appointment? Because if you're on a schedule, you can examine Banjo while I tend to Fudge."

"No more appointments today. I'll get the grooming tote and help you with Fudge. My horse, after all."

"He's also part of the family. I don't mind keeping track of him for you."

"I appreciate that." Wes walked into the six-stall barn. Seemed tiny after the Lazy S. He located the grooming tote in a cubby that served as a pseudo tack room. Quite a change from the layout his dad had owned in Spokane.

They worked in tandem as they had for years on the Lazy S. Wes put away Fudge's saddle and blanket while his dad brushed the dust and sweat from the gelding's coat. Since that was a one-person job, Wes leaned against the barn and asked about the latest scratchboard project.

"It's coming along. You can check it out after we're done here."

"I'd love to." The talented song of a mockingbird drifted from somewhere out behind the house. A breeze sighed through the tops of the pines surrounding the house and barn. Peaceful. So different from the hustle-bustle of the Lazy S. "I gathered from what Pete was saying yesterday that he's happy with his job."

"He loves it. His boss is a single lady."

"No kidding? I didn't know that."

"Pete said she got the ranch as part of a divorce settlement. She doesn't know much about ranching but she wants to learn."

"She has the right foreman, then."

"Pete says she's nice. I haven't met her yet."

"I'm glad he landed in a good spot. Oh, and I found out from Michael yesterday that their new house should be done by September."

"Fingers crossed it's before snow flies. I think it will be, though. Everybody's on a good trajectory except..."

"Gage." Wes was always reluctant to introduce the subject, but his dad seemed to want the conversation to go in that direction. "What do you hear from him?" He couldn't remember the last time he'd talked to Gage. A phone call on his birthday. That might have been it.

"He lets me know when he's moved from one job to another." His dad finished with the brush and picked up a towel for a final wipe-down. "Mostly it's on a ranch, but if he can't get that he hires on with a construction crew or tends bar. He calls himself a Renaissance Man."

"Fancy name."

"Fancy name for a guy who doesn't know what the hell he wants from life. He worries me. Gage is the only one of you kids who makes me flinch these days."

"Has he said whether he's planning to check out the new homestead?"

"Not specifically. I told him we packed up a couple boxes of the stuff he'd left at the Lazy S. He promised to come fetch it, but didn't say when."

"Well, it's the start of the busy season for ranchers. He probably wants to make that money while he can."

"Could be. I just wish…" He shrugged and returned the towel to the grooming tote. "Let's go see what Banjo has to say for himself."

Banjo had a simple sprain and Wes recommended keeping his foreleg wrapped for a day or so. After he finished up with Banjo, he walked with his dad to the studio. The new project was in the beginning stages, but he had no trouble recognizing that it was a life-sized rendering of a large eagle's nest, complete with mother, father and a couple of eaglets.

"Dad, you can't let some tourist buy this and cart it back East somewhere. It needs to stay in this town."

"I had the same thought this morning. I think it belongs in the Raptors Rise lobby."

"Great idea."

"But I don't want Zane buying it. He has more critical line items in his budget. I'll donate it to the cause, but that leaves me with no large piece to hang in the empty spot at the GG. Michael likes having something there now that folks are used to it."

"Then how about this? Put it up on the wall at the GG with a *Not for Sale* sign, just so the wall's not blank. Then tell Zane you'll be donating it to his organization as soon as you've created another large piece to go in its place."

His dad nodded. "That could work. In fact, we could hang a little sign beside it explaining where it will go and promoting Raptors Rise."

"You might want to make prints of different sizes for the Country Store. And it's a natural for those note cards Roxanne's had printed up."

"Yeah." He grinned. "It is. You'd think I would have considered all that when I decided to create this, wouldn't you?"

"You didn't?"

"No, sir. It just seemed like a challenging project with the texture of the nest and the bird feathers and all." He glanced at a small clock on his desk. "Yikes, I need to motate. I'm due to pick up Kendra in thirty minutes."

"For what?"

"Seeing a movie in Bozeman tonight."

"Cool. Have fun."

"We always do. Hey, thanks for coming out to check on Banjo. Let me know if you and Ingrid decide to go riding."

"I will." He hugged his father goodbye and headed out to his truck.

He had to smile as he drove back to town. He'd been prepared to accept an invitation to dinner or at least a beer on the porch. But his dad had made plans with his lady.

After standing by for years watching his kids fall in and out of love, it was his turn and Wes was the one with a free evening. Yesterday he'd exchanged phone numbers with Ingrid, so on impulse he pulled into the parking lot of the Eagles Nest Diner and texted her. *I owe you a thank you for this morning's shower. I'm at the diner. How about if I order dinner and bring it over?*

She might be reluctant after the weird way they'd ended the previous night. Then again, she might not. He still didn't know what her quick kiss had meant. Maybe during dinner he could find out. He only had to wait a few minutes for her reply. *That would be nice. Thanks.*

After a exchange of texts to find out what she wanted, he climbed out of his truck and walked into the diner.

Twenty minutes later he was driving home. He parked and took the stairs quickly with his bags of food. He stopped by his apartment long enough to ditch his keys, wallet and hat. Grabbing a couple of beers out of the fridge, he made tracks for her apartment and gave a quick rap on the door.

She came to the door in bare feet, a pair of sweats and an old t-shirt. Her hair was pinned on top of her head but was starting to come down.

She looked beautiful.

"Thanks for bringing dinner." She stepped back so he could come in, although she didn't hold his gaze for long.

The TV was on. "Whatcha watching?"

"The Food Network."

He chuckled. "Of course you are. And likely getting hungry while you waited for me to show up with dinner."

"Not a problem. I'll turn it off." She picked up the remote.

"You don't need to. I've never watched the Food Channel before. Is it interesting?"

"This one is. It's a competition to see who can build the tallest layer cake without it falling over."

"I'd like to watch that." He put the bags on the coffee table in front of her sofa. She'd already brought out plates and silverware. "Want one of these beers?"

"Better not so close to my bedtime. Like you said last night, one beer and I'll fall over. But the food smells delicious. Thank you."

"You're so welcome." He started pulling out the containers. "I haven't been home all day. Did you happen to notice whether a plumber was here?"

He glanced up when she didn't respond right away. Were her cheeks a little pink?

"He was here. I saw the truck about two this afternoon, so I stopped the guy before he left around three. He said you were all set." She dished her food onto a plate. "This salad looks great. Tomatoes are finally in season." She glanced at his dinner. "Not a salad guy?"

"Not especially. It's okay but I'd rather have fries." He smiled at her. "I'm glad you were free for dinner. Having someone to eat with is nice."

"Uh-huh." She hadn't met his gaze since he'd come into the apartment and she was definitely blushing.

Was she embarrassed because she'd caught him in the hallway in just a towel? The unexpected encounter had tripped him up at the time but he'd gotten over it when he'd noticed the expression on her face. It had done wonderful things for his ego. Maybe if the situation had been reversed, he'd be the one reacting more like she was doing.

Mentioning it wouldn't help, though, so he sat down.

"I'm going to get some water." She ducked into her kitchen nook and came back with a full glass. Then she settled down on the far end of the sofa and picked up her plate.

He followed her lead. "I'm starving. I skipped breakfast and didn't have much for lunch, either."

"Then I'm glad you're having a good dinner."

"Thanks for sharing it with me." He tucked into his meal while he watched the cake towers rising on the screen. Then one tower tilted and went down. "Wow. Good thing they gave each contestant a lot of room for fallout. What a mess."

"That's the appeal."

"I can see that." He continued to eat as the other three contestants added more layers. He glanced at her. "Is your food okay?"

"Mm-hm."

But she hadn't polished off much of her meal and he was nearly finished. He didn't remember her being a slow eater yesterday. When he'd cleaned his plate, he set it on the coffee table and picked up his beer. "Are you sure the food tastes okay?"

"It tastes fine. And I appreciate you bringing it. I'm just not very hungry."

He frowned. "I'm confused. If you weren't hungry, why did you agree to have me bring dinner?"

"Because—" She glanced at the TV and picked up the remote. "Do you mind if I turn this off?"

"Go right ahead."

After clicking the remote, she swiveled so she was facing him. "I thought it would be a good time to talk and I was hoping I could eat, but..." She shrugged.

She was clearly upset. If he hadn't been so focused on food when he'd arrived, he might have noticed earlier. He put down his beer. "Is this about last night? Or this morning?"

Pink tinged her cheeks again. "This morning was just a crazy accident." Her gaze skittered away.

"I never dreamed you'd come upstairs."

"I forgot you might be in the shower." She swallowed. "It's not important. It's not like it will ever happen again."

"True." Although unless he'd lost all his powers of observation, that meeting in the hall this morning had affected her. She might want it to happen again, whether she'd admit it or not.

"Anyway, last night I said I'd explain about the poster and I—"

"You don't have to."

"Yes, I do." She hesitated. "Especially after last night. I kissed you."

"I noticed."

"But I shouldn't have." Her color was still high.

"Why not?"

"Because I just broke up with my boyfriend. He cheated."

Ouch. "That explains the poster. How long ago did you break up?"

"Three weeks."

"Three weeks?" That wasn't very long. No wonder her emotional reactions were topsy-turvy. "Is he in town?"

"He's in Boston."

"Ah."

"The point is, I'm kind of a mess right now."

"I can understand that." Unfortunately, she was also tempting as hell.

She looked at him with her Caribbean blue eyes. "Could we just forget about that kiss?"

Not on your life. "I'll do my best."

"Good. That's good. And, um, I hate to be a bad hostess, but...it's past my bedtime."

"Right." Now there was a loaded subject. He picked up his empty plate. "I'll just—"

"You can leave it. I'll clean up."

"Oh. Okay." He put it down again. "I'll grab this stuff and get out of your way." He gathered the food containers and his empty beer bottle before stuffing them in the bag.

"Thank you for dinner."

"Anytime." He picked up the bag and the unopened beer. "Thanks for the company." Flashing her a smile, he headed out the door.

He was glad she'd told him about the ex. It gave him a much better idea of where he stood, and explained why she was sending mixed signals. She was clearly attracted to him, but it was perfectly natural that she'd resist that attraction so soon after a breakup. That was fine. He had all the time in the world.

8

Having Wes in her apartment had been unsettling, but Ingrid was ultimately pleased with how the discussion had gone. She'd cleared the air and now they could move forward as friends.

That was important because she enjoyed being with him. He gave off good energy. His parting smile stayed with her as she cleaned up the dishes and got ready for bed.

She slept better than she had since her Boston trip. She woke up in a good mood, roused from a lovely dream, but she lost the thread of it when her alarm chimed.

Then she stepped in the shower, where the pine fragrance of his shampoo lingered, and her dream came back in vivid color. *Oh, my.* Her subconscious and her libido had partnered for quite the episode involving Wes.

But sultry dreams about Wes were a vast improvement over the icky nightmares about Mark she'd been having for the past three weeks. As long as she didn't act on those dreams, her fantasy life was nobody's business.

The morning rush was in full flood when Wes came into the bakery around eight. She didn't wait on him, thank goodness. Doug handed him a to-go cup of coffee and Abigail rang that up along with his pastry.

Before he left carrying both items, he called out "'Morning, Ingrid!" and sent a smile in her direction.

"'Morning, Wes!" She ducked her head to hide her blush, but the brief interchange still gave her a lift.

Her upbeat mood lasted through the day. For dinner, she heated up the leftovers from what he'd brought her the night before. His truck hadn't been in its parking spot when she'd come upstairs so he was probably helping a client. Or over at his dad's place.

Then her phone pinged with a text message. *On my way home. I have something for you if you'll be around.*

That was two nights in a row he'd decided to bring her something. *What is it?*

A surprise. See you in about 10.

She loved surprises. Always had, ever since she'd been a kid. But this one made her nervous. Ten minutes seemed like twenty. The rhythmic sound of his boots on the stairs was her signal to walk out of her apartment and head him off. Whatever he had planned would be easier to deal with in the hallway.

He stepped around the corner holding a medium-sized produce basket filled with glossy ripe tomatoes—heirlooms judging from the varied colors. When he caught sight of her, his expression brightened. "Hey, there."

"Is that the surprise?"

"This is it."

As surprises went, it was a good one. She'd been afraid he was bringing flowers. Or something else that signaled romance. Tomatoes definitely did not. "They're gorgeous. Where did you get them?"

"I passed a stand on my way home and these were sitting right out front. You'd mentioned tomatoes last night, so I stopped."

He'd remembered. That was...sweet. "Were they selling them by the basket?"

"No, but I bought it, too, because they were so pretty arranged in it. They seemed startled that I wanted the whole thing."

"I'll bet." He'd probably created quite a stir. "There are a lot here. I assume we're going to share?"

"I'll take a couple. My guess is you like them way more than I do, so you can have the rest."

"Then let me pay for—"

"Nope. My idea. My treat."

It was a generous impulse. She didn't want to hurt his feelings by rejecting his gift. "Well, thank you. I'll give some to Abigail. She loves fresh tomatoes as much as I do." She took the basket. "Which two do you want?"

"These look good." He picked out a yellow and a red. "I also wanted to ask you about riding. You said you'd like to go. Are you still interested?"

She blinked. She'd completely forgotten that conversation.

Riding would be wonderful. Other than the trip down Main Street, she hadn't been on a horse in years. And his attitude tonight was casual and relaxed. He was acting like a good friend. Apparently explaining her situation had accomplished her goal. Which meant she was free to go riding with him. "Sure."

"How about this Sunday, then? The weather looks good and Pete has to work so Clifford's available."

"Sunday sounds great."

"Then let's do it. Kendra's trail rides will be going out, but we'll just take a different route. Morning or afternoon?"

"Morning, if that works for you."

"I'll make sure it does." His phone chimed. "Whoops. Can you take these back for a sec?" He returned both tomatoes to the basket, pulled his phone from his pocket and put it to his ear. "Hey, Floyd, what's up?" He frowned. "Yes, sir. I'll head out, now. See you soon."

"Problems?"

"A foal that's not doing well. If you don't mind putting those two tomatoes in my apartment, I'd—"

"Be glad to."

"Great. I'll text once I talk to Kendra about Sunday."

"Okay."

"Later." He touched the brim of his hat and clattered down the stairs.

"Good luck!" she called after him.

"Thanks!"

* * *

Ingrid didn't see Wes again until he arrived at her door on Sunday morning. His hair was still damp from the shower and the scent of pine drifted in her direction. He stood in the doorway with his hat in one hand and a bag of baby carrots in the other.

"Carrots for the horses?"

"Unless you have a hankering for some."

She laughed. "Not really."

"Then looks like the horses get 'em."

"I'm sure they'll love that." She stepped back from the door. "Come on in. I'll get my hat. I didn't want to put it on until I saw the whites of your eyes."

He pulled a long face. "You doubted me? You cut me to the quick."

"Oh, I didn't doubt that you *wanted* to be here, but you could have had an emergency, or you could have been so exhausted you overslept."

"I did oversleep," he called after her. "I need to come up with a better alarm on my phone. Fortunately, I'm a ninja at getting ready fast."

"I'm sure that comes in handy," she replied as she pulled her hair through the hole in the back of her Guzzling Grizzly baseball cap that matched her black t-shirt. Then she shoved money in her pocket in case they stopped to eat later. No need to take a key.

He gestured toward the open door with his hat. "After you."

As they walked down the hall, she glanced at him. "I decided not to bring my phone. Do you have yours?"

"Always."

"What if a client calls you while we're on the ride?"

"That shouldn't happen." He followed her down the stairs. "I put a message on my phone directing any emergency calls to the equine clinic in Three Forks. They can field anything major that comes in this morning."

"Good thinking. I'm glad you set that up."

"I had to, for this ride and for the future. Otherwise, I'd be forever chained to my phone and vehicle. It's less than an hour to Three Forks. Until I set up my practice, the clinic there was the closest option for folks in Eagles Nest. My clients love having me nearby and on call twenty-four-seven, but..."

"That's not sustainable."

"You know, it might be once the first flurry of excitement dies down and everyone gets to know me." They stepped into bright sunshine and he settled his hat on his head. "Some have admitted they called me out to their place to size me up and make sure I'd do."

"Like a trial run?"

"Kind of." He pushed the button on his keychain to unlock the doors on his black pickup. "They generally ask about some minor thing that will likely get better on its own. They know it and I know it. When I confirm that we should just let it be and I only charge them the minimum, I pass the test." He opened the passenger door and helped her in.

Coming around to the driver's side, he tucked the bag of carrots behind the seat before he climbed in. The truck's cab became an intimate space, indeed.

"Want the windows up or down?"

"Down, please. It's a beautiful day." And she might be less aware of the clean, masculine scent she found so appealing.

"It's a gorgeous day." After powering down the windows, he backed out of the parking space and drove through town, passing the Guzzling Grizzly on the way. "Every time I go by the GG I think of the night back in March when we were there with Roxanne and everyone helped invent the Guzzling Grizzly shooter."

She laughed. "That was a wild night."

"Last time I was in there I forgot to look and see if it was still on the menu."

"Probably is, but I can't say for sure. Professional bakers make lousy party animals."

"So do equine vets. I keep thinking I'll pop in on a Friday or Saturday evening for drinks and dancing, but emergencies seem to happen on the weekend for some reason."

"How's that foal, the one you were going off to see on Friday night?"

"He'll be fine. I checked in with them this morning so they'd know I'll be out of touch."

"That was nice."

"They're sweet people. The mare had a difficult pregnancy and so they were worried that the foal would end up with issues. He didn't, but whenever he so much as sneezed, they started to panic. Having me there to monitor the situation for a few hours Friday night made them feel better."

"Like a warm blankie."

"Guess so. Sometimes that's the biggest part of the job. And the scariest, in some ways. I've been trained in veterinarian medicine, but I'm not a magician. I try to tell folks that, but I'm not sure they hear me."

"Because they don't want to. They want to believe you'll ride in and save the day, like the Lone Ranger."

He chuckled. "Yeah, right."

"You need a mask."

"When I was a kid I had one."

"Yeah?"

"It's funny that you mentioned the Lone Ranger. That's who I wanted to be when I grew up. I begged Dad to get a white horse, which he wasn't about to do. I talked Roxanne into dressing up as Tonto one Halloween."

"I'll bet you were a cute little devil in your mask and white hat."

"I was mighty impressed with myself, that's for sure. Outgrew the white hat and haven't owned one since. Totally impractical."

"But what a great system. Bad guys wore black hats and good guys wore white hats. You never got confused as to who was the hero."

He flashed her a grin. "Is my black hat confusing you?"

"Not at all. You're Roxanne's brother and Quinn's son. There's no way you could be anything but a good guy."

When he looked over at her, his gaze was several degrees warmer than it had been earlier. "Glad you think so."

Her breath caught. *Holy cow.* Her *only friends* assumption had just gone up in smoke.

9

Was he a good guy? Wes was in no position to judge. She'd seemed startled by the look he'd given her. He'd have to be more careful. If she put him in the same league as his dad, that was high praise. He didn't want to tarnish his image.

He slowed the truck as he drove down the dirt road to his dad's place. No point in kicking up dust, even if his truck was already coated with it. A dusty exterior was one of the consequences of driving out to ranches at all hours of the day and night.

Ingrid surveyed the ranch house as it came into view. "Looks inviting with the rockers on the porch and the flowers."

"Way better than it did when Dad bought it. He and Pete have done a terrific job sprucing it up." He parked the truck, reached behind the seat for the carrots, and climbed down.

The four rocking chairs on the porch had been evenly spaced Thursday night, but since then two had been scooted together so they almost touched. Clearly his dad and Kendra had done some porch-sitting. Made him smile.

Ingrid was already out of the truck by the time he reached the passenger side. She glanced up at him, her face shadowed by the bill of the GG cap. "You said Pete had to work today, but is your dad around?"

The cap added a cuteness factor that made him want to put his arms around her and cuddle her. "Dad's here, but he's not receiving visitors."

"Is he sick?"

"He's working. Mornings are when he heads to his studio."

"Where is it?"

"Down that path, behind the house."

"Does he work there every morning?"

"Pretty much. Especially like now when he's involved in a project he's eager to finish. See that yellow bandana tied on the front doorknob?"

She looked over. "Oh, yeah. I didn't notice it before."

"That's a signal that he's out back and not to be disturbed."

"Good signal."

"Subtle but effective. He came up with it after he and Kendra invented the red bandana signal for her front door."

"And why would...oh." Her cheeks grew a little pink and she glanced away.

She looked even cuter when she blushed. "They had to come up with something and neither of them liked the idea of locking the door. This way anyone can see the bandana from the yard and they don't even bother to try the door."

She still didn't look at him. "Ingenious."

"I thought so."

She gazed across the property in the direction of Wild Creek Ranch. "Your dad and Kendra have such an interesting arrangement. Do you think they'll ever live together?"

"I don't know. They both have such big personalities that they might always need the independence of living apart."

"It seems to be working for them. And I guess it would make getting together more special."

"That's the way it looks to me." Now if he could just get *her* to look at him. "Ready to saddle up?"

That did it. "I sure am." She fell into step beside him as he started toward the barn, her body language more relaxed. "How different is this place from the one in Spokane?"

"Night and day. Dad had two eighteen-stall barns on the Lazy S. This one has only six stalls. There's one corral here and he had three before, plus a lot of acreage in fenced pastureland."

"Really big, then."

"It was, but the main difference is the activity level. Horses, people, and pickups were always in motion. Kendra has plenty happening at Wild Creek, too, but nothing compared to the Lazy S."

"It sounds exhausting."

"I'm sure it was, although he wouldn't admit it. He's clearly happy to be out from under the responsibility, though. It's a wonder he could create his art in that atmosphere. This has to be better for—" A high-pitched whinny came through the open doors of the barn. "On my way, Fudge! Hang on, buddy."

"He knows you're coming?"

"Yeah. It's touching how he still calls out to me even though he doesn't see me much. When I was in school, I tried to make it up to him in the summer. This time I'll just have to wait until things settle down a bit." He paused outside the open barn door. "Want to take some carrots?"

"Love to. Thanks."

He divided them with her and pocketed his half. "I want to check on Banjo's leg before we take the other two out. Come on down with me so you can meet him."

"You bet."

He ushered her into the cool interior of the barn. Clifford, Fudge and Banjo stuck their heads out to see what was going on. "Gotta check on the Banjo-man first, guys. Hang tight."

"Your dad's Harley's looking good."

Pausing at the stall where the motorcycle was parked, he smiled. "Yeah, he keeps it polished so it'll look sharp whenever he and Kendra go for a ride." He continued down the aisle. "Hey, Banjo, how's your sore leg, buddy?"

Banjo nickered a greeting.

"I'd like you to meet my friend Ingrid. She brought you carrots." He winked at her.

She laughed, just as he'd hoped she would. "Actually your buddy Wes here brought the carrots." She pulled one out of her pocket and held it on her level palm. "I'm just the delivery method." Her smile widened as the gelding nuzzled her hand. "I'd forgotten how much fun this is. Can I give him another one?" She looked like a kid in a candy store. Or in her case, a bakery.

"Sure. Then I'll go in and check his leg." Her delight in dispensing carrots was an unexpected bonus. She was clearly meant to spend time with horses and he was just the guy to facilitate that program.

After confirming that Banjo was nearly healed, he waited while Ingrid fed him another carrot. Then he gave the buckskin one last pat and headed toward Fudge and Clifford.

"Clifford, my man, you remember Ingrid, right? You two met during the parade. She wants to get to know you better. And she has carrots."

"I sure do." Ingrid approached the big roan without hesitation. In no time, she was stroking his nose, feeding him carrots and scratching under his forelock. "We're going to be great friends, you and me."

"I can tell he likes that idea."

"So do I." She looked over at him. "What about Fudge?"

"Right." Caught staring at her like a doofus. He turned to his horse, who was giving him the hairy eyeball. "Sorry, buddy," he murmured as he fed the bay carrots and stroked his silky neck. "Got distracted."

"I'm out of carrots," Ingrid said.

"Me, too. I'll get the lead ropes."

"Can I lead Clifford out?"

"Absolutely." He came back with the ropes and handed her one.

"I might need a refresher course on saddling and bridling him, though. It's been a few years."

"You don't have to tack him up. I can—"

"But I want to! That's half the fun. You get to know the horse better that way."

"True." Every move she made and every comment she uttered endeared her to him more and more. And made him want to find a way past the emotional barriers she kept shoving into place. Good thing her ex was in Boston. Wes had the urge to knock the guy into next week.

Once they had both horses tethered to the hitching rail he fetched the grooming tote. He handed her one brush and he took another. Then he was treated to her soft murmurs as she talked to Clifford while she groomed him.

Usually he talked to Fudge, too, but he didn't want to block out the sound of Ingrid's voice so he kept his mouth shut. It was sweet torture, listening to her croon to the horse as she stroked his silky coat. And it had a predictable effect on the region just below Wes's belt buckle. He ignored the temporary discomfort, soaking up the picture she made standing beside the big roan.

Before she finished brushing Clifford, he headed into the barn to fetch the tack and to give himself a moment to cool down. She was more potent than one of her Firecrackers, and she didn't even know it.

Stepping back into the sunshine, he set the saddle on the railing and looped the bridle over the eye bolt attached to one of the posts.

She looked the tack over. "Maybe I can do it myself, after all. But you should probably supervise."

She was giving him permission to watch her every move? He wasn't about to pass that up. "Okay." He stood with arms folded and did his best to pay attention to what she was doing and not how adorable she looked doing it. Thankfully he didn't have to say a word as she saddled Clifford with the efficiency of a seasoned hand.

She stood back with a smile of satisfaction. "Guess I'm not as rusty as I thought."

"Not rusty at all."

"Is this Pete's saddle?"

"Yes, but technically it's Clifford's saddle. Dad taught us that the saddle should fit the horse first and the rider second. You may find this one a little roomy."

"No worries. I'll adjust the stirrups."

"Need help?"

"Thanks, but I have a pretty good eye."

Among other things. After observing her in this setting, he didn't doubt she could handle the adjustments. "Then I'll leave you to it while I tack up Fudge." He couldn't risk her catching him staring. By the time he finished, she'd exchanged Clifford's halter for a bridle and mounted up.

He grinned at her. "Looks like somebody's ready to ride."

"You'd better believe it. If I were any more excited, I'd burst into flames like baked Alaska."

He ducked his head and pretended to adjust the girth on Fudge's saddle. He didn't want her to see his reaction to *that* particular comment.

"Then let's do this thing." He glanced up at the sky where the clouds had mostly blocked the sun. "Those clouds are coming in a little early. The rain's not predicted until later in the day."

"I was watching them, too."

He looked at her. "Will it be a problem if it starts falling before we make it back?"

"Not for me. I won't melt."

"Then let's head out." He swung into the saddle and touched his heels to Fudge's smooth flanks. "Come on up beside me. We can ride abreast until we get to the highway." Which was an added treat for him.

"Thank you for bringing me out here." She urged Clifford forward with a soft click of her tongue. "I hadn't realized how much I miss being around horses."

"Have you ever had one of your own?"

"No. My mom and I didn't live in an area where you could keep a horse on the property and she was dead-set against the idea of me boarding one."

"That's a bummer." No mention of a dad. He tucked that information away for future consideration.

"It was at the time, but in hindsight, it would have been a disaster. I would have had to finance it all on my own, including boarding, buying tack, vet bills...it was more than I could have handled, no matter how many jobs I got after school."

"And if you'd taken extra jobs to pay for the horse, you wouldn't have had time to ride."

"That was always the catch. Briefly I thought of working on a ranch to get my horse fix, but that didn't feel like what I wanted to do for the rest of my life. I think I've always known my career would involve food."

"You followed your bliss."

"Yes, I did." At the same moment that she turned to him and smiled, the sun broke through the clouds, surrounding her with golden light.

He pulled his horse to a stop and sat very still, unable to tear his gaze away. She was the most beautiful woman he'd ever seen.

Ingrid pulled Clifford to a stop, too. She looked over at him, clearly puzzled. "Wes? Is something wrong?"

No. Everything's perfect. But if he told her she'd dazzled him with her beauty, he'd scare her away. "No." He paused to clear his throat to buy some time. What could he say that wouldn't be an out-and-out lie? "I was just thinking about..." He couldn't come up with a single thing.

"Your clients?"

Yes! Perfect. But a lie if he agreed. He gave a non-committal shrug.

"Darn it, I was afraid you'd have trouble putting it out of your mind."

"Force of habit. Won't happen again." Although he'd be picturing her caught in the glow of the sunlight for days, months...maybe even years to come.

"It's honorable that you care so much, Wes. But you don't want to be consumed by your job."

"You're right. That would be tragic." And he needed to get her off this topic before he dug himself into a hole. "How about planning to ride with me again next Sunday morning? It'll force me to focus on something other than work." *Like you.*

Something flickered in her gaze. "I'd like that."

"Good. Me, too." And he'd like it even more if she kept looking at him that way.

<u>10</u>

If Wes had been distracted by his work before, he certainly wasn't now. He was focusing one hundred percent of his attention on her. And warming her from the inside out.

He'd looked amazing wearing only a towel, but he looked damn good on his horse, too. The two visuals were competing for dominance in her brain. Unfortunately, she shouldn't be considering either one, not if she was determined to maintain her distance.

Only friends, only friends, only friends. It would be her mantra. She nudged Clifford back into a walk. "Did you get a chance to eat breakfast before you left your apartment this morning?"

He walked Fudge beside her. "No. It turns out I'd rather sleep than eat. Besides, the bakery was closed."

"You could have stocked food in your apartment."

He grinned. "I could, but where's the fun in that?"

She smiled back. "I shouldn't say this, considering my profession, but a regular diet of coffee and pastries for breakfast isn't particularly healthy."

"It's an improvement from my college days. I didn't live above a bakery, then. Breakfast, even coffee and a pastry, hardly ever happened."

She made a tsking noise. "With the long hours you put in, you need food, After this ride, how about we get lunch?" And she was only asking because she was concerned for his welfare. Really.

"You're on."

She glanced at his friendly, relaxed smile, and her stomach did a flip. Not a good sign. "What sort of instructions did you get from Kendra about our ride trajectory?"

"We're supposed to go past the barn, through the pasture and out the gate on the far side. If we take the path to the right, we won't run into her trail riders."

"Good deal." She glanced around. "The last time I was on this road, Abigail and I were delivering Faith and Cody's wedding cake to the ranch house."

"And my dad was on his way to Eagles Nest to announce his intentions to Kendra."

"He showed up without an invitation. Epic move."

"That's my dad. King of the epic moves."

"You're no slouch in that department, carrying me over the finish line." She'd replayed that scene several times. Okay, maybe a dozen.

"It seemed like the thing to do." The breeze picked up and he tugged on the brim of his hat. "That race was a blast. The tug of war was, too."

"I like the tug of war, but I like the race better."

"Yeah, me, too. It's harder than it looks."

"That's what catches people up. They think *how hard can it be*?"

"Guilty. But I'll be better prepared next year. I miss being involved in physical competition. In college we played flag football when the weather was warm enough."

"Sounds like fun."

"It was. I wonder if I could talk some of the guys into playing a game now and then, maybe midweek, early evening. Depending on the weather, we could probably play into October."

"What about coed?"

"Sure, why not?" He looked over at her. "Would you do it?"

If he was playing? "Absolutely. My job mostly involves standing so I could use the exercise. I don't know much about football, but—"

"I do. You'd pick it up in no time. Pete would go for it. I'll bet some of the McGavin brothers would, too. My dad and Kendra might even want in."

She grinned. "They already have the right shoes."

"Yeah, they do. That might be a trick, getting the other guys into gym shoes."

"Maybe not, now that Quinn and Kendra won the three-legged race. I can see Rox wanting to play, too."

"Yeah, she would. Good call. I'm liking this idea. Coed would make it more fun. Thanks for suggesting it." He gazed at her. "And thanks for coming with me today."

"Thanks for inviting me."

Moments later, the ranch house came into view. Kendra waved to them from the porch and Wes turned Fudge in that direction. "Let's go say hello before we head out."

"Definitely."

Kendra came down the porch steps and out to the end of the walk to greet them. She glanced up at Ingrid. "You look right at home on Clifford."

"We're getting along great."

"How did I not know that you liked to ride? I would have asked you out here if I'd realized that."

"I just didn't think about it, I guess. I haven't ridden since I left home. Got out of the habit." Mark had never shown an interest, so she'd kind of forgotten about it.

"Well, anytime you have the urge, I'd be glad to trade you a ride for a dozen brownies."

"Thanks. I'll remember that."

"I'm hoping she'll make these Sunday rides with me a regular thing," Wes said.

"That would be nice." Kendra smiled, but her expression underwent a subtle change as she looked between the two of them.

Uh-oh. Leave it to Kendra to pick up on emotional undercurrents. And here Ingrid thought she'd been hiding her reactions to Wes so well. She did her best to sound nonchalant. "I'll have to see how it goes. Sometimes Abigail needs me to bake with her on Sundays."

Kendra nodded. "That I know. Luke has to work around those emergency pie-baking sessions when he wants to ride with Abigail." She turned to Wes. "And speaking of pies, did you see all the comments on that picture of you smeared with cherry juice?"

"I did. Who knew folks preferred an undignified vet?"

"I could have told you that. I'm partial to that quality, myself. Anyway, I'm glad you found time to fit in a ride today."

"Me, too. The celebration on the Fourth reminded me how much I miss being on the back of a horse."

"And playing football," Ingrid said. "On the way over we talked about setting up some coed flag football games. Do you think anyone would be interested?"

"You know, they might. Ryker and Zane both played in high school. I can see April and Mandy going for it."

"What about you and Quinn?"

She blinked. "Are you thinking multigenerational, then?"

"Hey, you guys won the three-legged race. You can hang. That goes for the Whine and Cheese ladies, too. I say we throw it open to everybody."

"Sounds like fun. Want me to pass the word, see what response I get?"

"That would be awesome."

"I'll do that, then." She looked up at the sky. "If you two want to fit in your ride before the rain starts, you'd better take off."

"Yes, ma'am." Wes touched the brim of his hat. "Thanks for letting us use your property."

"Anytime." She glanced at Ingrid. "I'll let you know about the flag football."

"Excellent."

"And like I said, bribe me with brownies and you can come out and ride anytime."

"You've got a deal."

* * *

Riding was good for so many things and Wes enjoyed all of them. Taking a horse down a trail on a solo trip gave him an excellent view of his surroundings and immersed him in the natural world he loved. Riding hell-bent-for-leather across an open field sent adrenaline pounding through his veins, pushing out any negative emotions and amplifying the positive ones.

But sharing the trail with another rider, in this case Ingrid, was his favorite time in the saddle. Trail riding invited good conversation. This was the perfect opportunity to get to know her better.

The cloud cover gave a softness to the landscape as they moseyed along side-by-side, accompanied by the clop of hooves, the creak of leather and the twitter of birds.

They'd discussed more details of the flag football project and he was tickled at how excited she was about it. "Did you play any sports in school?"

"Not really. We didn't have much money and taking up a sport requires at least some expense."

"True."

"I was way more interested in saving up for cake decorating lessons. One of the local ladies held classes in her home. I was always the youngest person there."

"And the most talented, I'll bet."

"Not at first. But I caught on fast."

"Where was that?"

"Miles City, about three and a half hours east of here. Ever been there?"

"No, ma'am, but then there's a lot of Montana I haven't seen. You mentioned your mom before. Is she..." He left the sentence dangling so she could fill in the blank.

"Still there. She doesn't get why I have all these dreams and schemes and I don't get why she's content to work a boring job forever. She says I inherited my ambition from my dad. He died in the service when I was a baby."

"That's too bad."

"It is. I think I would have liked him." She gave him a sideways glance. "Do you remember your mom at all?"

"I have some fuzzy memories. Dad says Roxanne is the spitting image of her, so now when I think of my mom, I'm probably picturing my sister."

"I can't imagine what that must have been like for your dad, being left with four young kids."

"I'm sure it was rough. I don't remember much about that time. I was barely four and

Roxanne was three. Pete was eight and Gage was six. I'm sure they were more aware of how Dad was taking it than I was."

"And what about Gage? I never hear about him."

"Because he's a mystery. Probably to himself, too. He stays on the move." He glanced ahead of them. "Speaking of moving, will you look at that? We've come to a big, wide meadow filled with wildflowers. Ready to canter across it?"

"Sure am."

"Then let's go." He gave a whoop and loosened the reins. Fudge took off.

Clifford did, too. The two horses behaved like a drill team, matching stride for stride. Wes glanced over at Ingrid. Cheeks flushed and smile wide, she radiated joy as she moved effortlessly with the horse.

He was riding through paradise with an angel. Life didn't get much better than this.

11

The clouds opened up as they crossed the paved road on the way back. Big, fat drops hit the brim of Ingrid's cap and she glanced over at Wes. "What do you want to do?"

He looked up at the clouds. "We could make a run for it, but we'll probably still get wet. Like I said, I don't mind a little rain."

"Me, either."

"Then let's just take it easy going back and accept the fact we'll get drenched."

"Works for me."

She was soaked to the skin by the time they rode past the house. The yellow bandana was still on the doorknob so Quinn must not have left his studio, yet. He might even find the patter of the rain inspiring.

Wes opened the barn doors and let her go first with Clifford. After he came in he tossed her several towels. She used the corner of one to wipe her face but couldn't see the point in drying the rest of her since she'd just get wet on the way back to the truck.

The tack got the benefit of the towels first. Wes came to fetch the saddle, bridle and damp saddle blanket while she used a sweat scraper to whisk the rainwater off Clifford's rump and neck. She grabbed one of the towels to wipe down his face, giving him a kiss on the muzzle when she finished. "Thanks for a great ride."

"Looking good."

She turned to find Wes standing in the doorway of the stall watching her. "Thanks."

He'd taken off his hat and he must have used a towel on his hair because it was going every which way.

The rain had soaked right through her hat, but she'd left it on to hold her ponytail in place. She'd wrung out her hair to keep it from dripping water down her back.

"That should do it." She gave Clifford one last swipe on his dark red coat before walking out of the stall and depositing the scraper in the grooming tote.

Wes closed the stall door behind her while she dumped the towel in a large bin with the others. She couldn't help smiling when she glanced at him. "Your hair's a hot mess." Much like it had looked when he'd come out of her apartment Thursday morning. His white Western shirt was nearly transparent as it clung to his broad chest.

"Yeah." He laughed as he ran his hands through his hair, causing it to stick up even more. "My presentation isn't the best right now."

"You've only made it worse. Here." Reaching up, she sank her fingers into his thick locks. *Oh. Ooohhh.* Her skin tingled and her breath caught as she finger-combed his damp hair into place.

His hand circled her wrist. ""Probably shouldn't do that." His voice was husky.

She met his gaze. The heat in his eyes could dry her off in no time. For one electric moment, she basked in it.

His eyes darkened. "Unless..."

Sanity prevailed. "No, I—" She backed away. "Sorry."

He released her wrist. "No worries." He shoved his hand in his pocket and cleared his throat. "We...um...talked about lunch."

"Yes! We did. Lunch." She was breathing too fast. So was he, and the way his wet shirt molded to his pecs was extremely distracting.

"There's the diner, but we're not exactly—"

"Diner-worthy." She glanced down at her shirt. It was plastered to her breasts, giving him a view much like hers. She immediately pulled the material away from her body and crossed her arms over her chest.

He glanced away. "Burger Barn?"

"Maybe. Although the drive-through takes forever, especially on Sunday."

"Okay. Then how about...um—"

"I have plenty of food at my place." Why the hell had she said that? Was she nuts? The pheromones flying between them must be impairing her judgment if she'd just invited him to her apartment.

"You're sure?" He studied her, clearly trying to figure this out.

She wished him luck with that. She didn't know why she'd made the offer either. But what was done was done. She'd calm the heck down after they got out of this charged situation. "Why not? It's convenient and I have food."

"Okay. The truck's unlocked, so we can just make a run for it. Ready?"

"Let's go."

He raced for the driver's side and she handled getting into the passenger seat. On the way back to town, he had to crack the windows and turn on the defroster when the windshield fogged up from the added moisture.

She didn't comment on it. She didn't want to call attention to their translucent clothing or the fact that they both seemed to be breathing a little funny. Everything would be fine once they reached their respective apartments and dried off.

The windshield wipers maintained a rhythmic beat in the otherwise silent cab. What to say, what to say? Food. She could talk about that. "I—"

"What—" His voice stumbled over hers. "Sorry. Go ahead."

"I was going to tell you what I was planning to fix."

"And I was going to ask."

"Veggie omelets, which will use up the last of the heirloom tomatoes. Did you eat yours, yet?"

"They're both still sitting there."

"Getting riper by the minute."

"Yes, ma'am." A muscle twitched in his jaw. "Sure are."

Either he was ramped up like she was or trying not to laugh. Could be either. "You might as well bring them after you get out of your wet clothes."

"I'll bring 'em." His voice sounded strange.

She peeked over at him. That slight dent in his cheek told her he was ready to bust out laughing. "What's so funny?"

"Nothing."

"No, really."

He took a quick breath. "Just getting past the image of striding buck naked down the hall, a ripe tomato in each hand."

She choked on a burst of startled laughter and spent the next minute trying to catch her breath. She didn't have any trouble generating that visual after the towel incident.

"Sorry. I guess you weren't picturing that."

"No." She dragged in a breath. "But I am, now, thank you very much."

"I can tell. Your face is about as red as a tomato."

"How attractive." She pressed her hands to her hot cheeks.

"It is, actually. Makes your eyes look really blue."

"Um, thanks." Butterflies danced in her stomach.

"Alrighty, then, veggie omelets. Sounds great."

"Good." She took another deep breath. "Do you like herbed potatoes?"

"I like potatoes any way I can get 'em."

"Then I'll fix those, too." His enthusiasm for food did nothing to lower the temperature in the truck.

"How can I help?"

"Help?"

"Absolutely. I'm not going to lounge on your sofa while you fix us lunch."

"Oh." That could complicate matters. If he stationed himself in her kitchen, the stove wouldn't be the only thing generating heat. "My kitchen's kind of small."

"Same size as mine, right?"

"Yes."

"Roxanne and I managed fine when I visited her in March."

"But she's your sister."

The corner of his mouth lifted. "Meaning what?"

Meaning I can't be that close to you without risking spontaneous combustion. "You've probably cooked together before." There. That sounded reasonable.

He glanced at her. "I'm sure we'll manage."

Good Lord, what had she gotten herself into? Sharing a meal was known territory. They'd done that the night he'd brought dinner.

But cooking together in her tiny kitchen? Preparing food was a sensual experience—the scents, the textures, the colors and the sounds. She resonated to the sizzle of onions in butter and the crunch of a red pepper under the blade of her knife. She couldn't imagine adding Wes to the mix without triggering an explosion.

"Rain's let up." He parked in front of the bakery and turned off the motor. "We won't have to make a dash for the door."

"That's good." But she didn't move.

He turned to face her. "Ingrid?"

"What?"

His voice gentled. "Do you *not* want me in your kitchen?"

Oh, she wanted him in her kitchen all right. In her kitchen, in her living room, in her bedroom...

Stop it! She had to get a grip before she spun out of control. Friends. They were supposed to be just friends, dammit! "It's fine."

"Because we can forget about having lunch together. I can eat one of those tomatoes—"

She gathered her courage. "I don't want to forget about it. Come down after you change clothes and we'll fix the omelets together."

"Should I bring my tomatoes?" Amusement danced in his dark eyes.

"Yes." God, he was tempting. And she was one small step away from raising the white flag. "One in each hand."

_12_

Out of necessity, Wes had perfected the art of a fast turnaround. A dry pair of jeans, a navy t-shirt left over from his college days, and he was ready to head down to Ingrid's apartment.

That might not be a good idea. In his experience, ladies took longer to change clothes, especially after getting rained on. Their hair was one factor. Ingrid might want to jump in the shower and rinse hers out before getting dressed.

Showing up five minutes after they'd parted in the hallway wouldn't be cool. He was desperately hungry, though, so he snacked on some mixed nuts to take the edge off.

Then he checked in with the clinic in Three Forks just in case. They had nothing to report. He considered calling the folks with the foal to make sure everything was fine, but that could backfire. Sure as the world, they'd ask him to come out the minute he was free. He didn't want to start something he wasn't prepared to finish.

Ten minutes later he headed out, holding a very ripe tomato in each hand. He cradled them as loosely as possible, although dropping them would be worse than squeezing them too tight. He should have eaten them before they turned into juice-filled grenades ready to spew everywhere.

That imagery conjured the buck-naked scenario he'd described earlier. He got distracted and tightened his grip on one of the tomatoes. His middle finger punctured the skin. It started leaking.

"Ingrid!" He stopped and did his best to lick the juice oozing between his fingers before it dripped on the floor. "I need a little help out here! Bring a bowl or something!"

A moment later she appeared in jeans and a t-shirt, her feet bare and a mixing bowl in her hand. "What the—oh, my God." She started laughing.

"Okay, okay." He kept licking. "Come quick before juice gets everywhere."

"Right." Still chuckling, she hurried over. "Just drop them—no, wait, *don't* drop..."

But he'd already let go and the tomatoes landed in the bowl with a splat. The bowl was deep enough to contain the juice, though. "Are they ruined?"

She glanced up at him. "Absolutely not. They can still go in the omelets. Or I can use them for tomato sauce, salsa, soup...lots of things."

But he wasn't hearing her words. He'd been captured by the effect of her golden lashes framing her incredible blue eyes as she gazed at him. He sighed. "You're amazing."

Her eyes widened. She swallowed. "Um, thank you." Her voice wasn't quite steady. And her cheeks were a little pink. "Lets...um...get these in the kitchen."

Unless he was imagining things, he was affecting her. That was good news. Because she was seriously affecting him. "I'm following you."

Carrying the bowl, she turned and started back toward her apartment. "I was grinding beans for coffee when you called for help."

He fell into step beside her. "Coffee would be great."

"I also forgot that I brought some cinnamon rolls upstairs yesterday. I thought we could have them with coffee while we're cooking, but you're welcome to have one with your omelet, too, if you want."

"I'd like that. Can't ever have too many." He followed her through the open door and into her kitchen. "I need to get the tomato juice off my hand. Then I'll be ready to help with whatever."

"Go for it."

After rinsing off at the sink, he dried his hands on a towel that hung nearby. Then he turned and watched her start their brew in her fancy-looking coffee maker. "Does that thing make lattes and stuff?"

"It does." She pushed a button and glanced up. "But you're a regular coffee guy so that's what I'm making."

"Must be kind of boring for you."

She gazed at him for a moment before turning away. "I'm not the least bit bored."

Whoa. The flash of fire in her eyes sent a message straight to his groin. "Good." The word came out a little raspy.

She opened the refrigerator. "I'll warm up the cinnamon rolls."

She'd warmed him up, that was for sure. And the tight quarters of her kitchen would accelerate the process. "What can I do?"

"Want to chop up some potatoes?"

No, I want to kiss your full pink mouth until neither of us can see straight. "Sure. Hand 'em over."

When she gave him the string bag of small, multi-colored potatoes, her fingers brushed his. Heat shot up his arm and his chest tightened like he'd touched a livewire. He hadn't anticipated making a move during this meal, but with all the electricity arcing between them, holding back might be a lot tougher than he'd expected.

She set him up next to the sink with a knife and a cutting board so he could rinse the potatoes as he worked. Normally he had a very steady hand, but it wasn't all that steady now.

The sweet, yeasty scent of warm cinnamon rolls filled the kitchen, along with the aroma of melted butter and whatever else she was sautéing in the frying pan where the potatoes were destined to go. His stomach growled but an even greater hunger was developing below his belt.

The woman who could satisfy both his desires was within reach, busily whisking eggs in a bowl. Was it possible to be in heaven and hell at the same time?

She set the bowl aside. "I'll get our coffee and cinnamon rolls."

"Excellent, thanks."

Moments later she put a full mug of coffee and a cinnamon roll on a plate next to him on the counter. "You must really like potatoes."

He evaluated the sizable mound on the cutting board and put down the knife before turning to her. "Or else I forgot what I was doing because I was distracted by you."

Surprise flickered in her eyes. "You were?"

"Yes, ma'am, but that's nothing new. I've been thinking about kissing you ever since that night in the hall. I've just been afraid to tell you."

"I see." A pulse beat in her throat as her attention drifted downward and lingered on his mouth.

That was a good beginning. "I think you've been thinking about it, too."

Her gaze lifted to his. The heat in her eyes confirmed it. "A kiss is…a big step."

"I know. That's probably why it's best if you're the one who takes it." He stood very still but his heart was going a mile-a-minute.

After an electric moment that seemed to last forever, she broke eye contact and drew in a shaky breath. "I need to start those potatoes." Picking up the cutting board, she turned toward the stove.

As the potatoes sizzled in the fragrant butter, Wes closed his eyes and willed his body to settle down. He wasn't wrong. She wanted him as much as he wanted her. But she didn't trust it. *Patience.*

A warm cinnamon roll with melted frosting was a poor substitute for kissing her, but eating it gave him something to do with his hands. And his mouth.

He turned around and leaned against the counter while he bit into it. "Thanks for the treat."

"You're welcome." She stood in front of the stove, her back to him as she tended the browning potatoes.

"Did you bake these?"

"I did, as a matter of fact."

"I thought so." Her royal blue t-shirt was the stretchy kind that hugged her curves. He was very aware of those curves. When she shifted her weight, the denim of her jeans tightened in response. So did his body.

She glanced over her shoulder. "There's no way you could tell Abigail's cinnamon rolls from mine. We work from the same recipe."

"I disagree. There's a slightly different shape. That goes for the bear claws, too."

"Hmm." She picked up her cinnamon roll and studied it. "Now I want to do a test and see if you really can tell." She leaned over the plate when the frosting started to drip. "I left these in a little too long."

"I like them this way. Gooey is good." Especially if it became a two-person experience.

"I guess I shouldn't be surprised you'd say that." She lowered the flame under the potatoes and put the lid on the pan before turning to face him. "I've never known anyone who enjoys sweets as much as you do."

"Neither have I, to be honest."

"You're a baker's dream come true."

"I only care about one particular baker." He sipped his coffee as he gazed at her over the rim of his mug. "I'm hoping my love of sweets gives us something in common."

She swallowed. "It does. But you can't live on sweets alone." She turned back to the stove. "I'm going to fix you the most delicious omelet you've ever tasted."

"Can't wait." She clearly wasn't ready to march over here and kiss him like there was no tomorrow, so he'd enjoy the heck out of her home-cooked meal. Considering the importance of food in her life, that was a significant gift.

And he'd be the most appreciative guest she'd ever welcomed to her table.

13

"Most delicious omelet ever." Wes pushed aside his plate after finishing the omelet and the cinnamon roll he'd added as dessert. He rested his muscled forearms on the table.

"Glad you think so." She'd barely tasted hers. She'd spent the entire meal in a heightened state of awareness of her dining companion. His encouragement to initiate a kiss lay like an invisible gauntlet on the table between them.

"Yes, ma'am." He took a breath, stretching the soft cotton of his t-shirt. "I don't say things I don't mean." His dark gaze held hers.

His words simmered in her brain. They were affecting the rest of her, too. "Good to know."

Sharing her intimate kitchen space following his kissing comment had been a stimulating experience, to say the least. The enticing aromas wafting from the stove and the visual of his toned body in snug jeans and a t-shirt had created a powerful distraction.

By some miracle, she hadn't set the kitchen on fire. She hadn't been nearly as successful keeping her internal thermostat under control. Now that the meal was over and he was gazing into her eyes, she was pushing into the red zone.

He laid his silverware on his plate. "I'll help you clean up."

"Okay."

But he didn't push back his chair. Neither did she.

Her heart beat so fast her ears started to ring. "Or..."

His eyes darkened. "Or?"

Was she really going to do this? Apparently she was. "Or...we could try that kiss."

The sexiest smile she'd ever seen curved his lips. "Yes, we could."

Drawn by the heat in his eyes and the promise in those lips, she rose from the table. He followed her up until they were standing a hair's breadth apart. She laid her hands on his warm chest, her palms absorbing the wild thumping of his heart through the soft cotton.

His breath hitched, but he didn't move a muscle. He'd told her this was her step to take. The look in his eyes made it clear he was giving her every chance to change her mind.

She wasn't going to. She wanted...this. Clutching his shoulders and lifting onto her toes, she closed her eyes and lightly touched her mouth to his.

His lips were warm and supple. Pulse racing, she began exploring, tasting buttercream frosting, cinnamon and tightly leashed desire. Only a slight tremor when she shifted her angle betrayed the passion lurking beneath his outward calm. He kept his arms at his sides.

Clearly he was still waiting, allowing her to set the pace. His restraint excited and intrigued her. Edging closer, she leaned into him as she slid her hands up the strong column of his neck. When she ran her fingers through the silky hair at his nape, he shivered.

Gradually she deepened the kiss as pleasure fizzed in her veins. With a soft groan, he wrapped her in his arms. His grip tightened, coaxing her closer, ever closer to the flames.

And she ignited, the flash fire sweeping through her. When he cupped the back of her head and thrust his tongue into her mouth, she whimpered with longing and pressed against the hard planes of his aroused body.

She'd known it would be like this. One kiss and she was already coming apart.

Backing her up against the table, he lifted her onto it. Dishes rattled. She wrapped her legs around his hips and wiggled closer, wanting all he had to give. As he continued to ravish her mouth, he reached under her shirt and unfastened the back clasp of her bra.

Then he lifted his mouth a fraction from hers. He was breathing hard. "Wait. I need…we can't—"

"What?" She gulped for air.

"This is…intense."

"I know." And a moment ago she'd been all for intense. But what he was saying slowly penetrated the thick, swirling fog of lust that had blotted out rational thought.

"We need to slow down."

She drew in a ragged breath. "You're right." Unwinding her legs from around his hips, she slid off the table as he stepped back and released her.

His chest heaved. "I didn't expect—"

"Me, neither."

"But—"

She found the courage to look at him. "We got carried away."

He held her gaze. "You say that like getting carried away was a bad thing."

"Not bad. It just…happened."

He massaged the back of his neck and gave her a smile that was close to a grimace. "This is not how I pictured our first kiss ending." He studied her for a moment. "What now?"

"I don't know." He was the one who'd pulled the plug, and she was grateful. In her current state, no telling how far she might have let things go. She still had the urge to haul him into her bedroom, but that wouldn't be fair—to either of them.

His expression softened as he gazed at her. "It was a heck of a good kiss."

Heat climbed into her cheeks, but she didn't look away. "Yes, it was." And she hoped they'd do it again sometime soon. When he'd thrust his tongue into her mouth—

"You need to stop looking at me like that."

His gentle words pulled her out of her daze. "Sorry."

"Don't be. But I only have so much willpower, and you're temptation personified."

She blinked. Temptation? Her? "Oh." It was a hard concept to wrap her mind around. Mark had certainly never described her that way.

"And that's why I should vamoose." He glanced at the table. "But I can still help with the clean-up—"

"I'll handle it." She needed time to think, and working in the kitchen would be the perfect opportunity.

"You're sure?"

"Yeah."

"Then I'll be off." He started toward the door.

"Wes?"

"Yes, ma'am?" He turned.

"Thank you. For the...kiss."

He smiled. "You're welcome." He walked out the front door, his retreating steps growing fainter, but there was no click of a closing door. She didn't close hers, either.

Cleaning up the kitchen gave her something to keep her body moving while her mind worked on more important matters.

She'd come darned close to letting her craving for physical contact sweep away her common sense after only one kiss. Her emotions were volatile and the pleasure she'd enjoyed in Wes's arms was a potentially dangerous catalyst.

So what was she going to do about it? Right now? Nothing. She needed time to process.

After the kitchen was shipshape, she tackled her usual Sunday chores. The familiar pattern soothed her, but it didn't prevent her from listening for Wes's footsteps.

She doubted he'd show up in her doorway—not after the noble way he'd handled their...encounter. But if he left the building, that would eliminate the temptation to walk down to his apartment and throw herself into his arms.

Temptation. That word held a whole new meaning for her now. She liked the glimpse of herself she'd gotten through his eyes. And her mini-obsession with Wes was perfectly natural after a kiss that still had the power to curl her toes. He'd given her time to think rationally about her situation, though, and she was determined to use it.

By bedtime she was calmer and more relaxed, although she still hadn't reached any conclusions about her next steps. As she set her alarm for three, her phone pinged with a message. *Sweet dreams, Ingrid.*

She tingled from head to toe as she typed a reply. *Same to you, Wes.* She crawled into bed and turned out the light. It was a small thing, maybe, that he wanted to wish her goodnight. But it warmed her like a hug. He was steps away, right down the hall. And he was thinking about her. Smiling, she drifted off to sleep.

At three she woke to her alarm and hopped in the shower. As she dressed, her phone pinged.

Got called out. Mare in labor. Didn't want you to worry.

She responded immediately. *Thanks for letting me know.* Poor guy wasn't likely to get the sleep he needed anytime soon.

For the next couple of days, they kept in touch via short texts. It was their only contact other than a quick wave when he came in for coffee and a pastry each morning. Unfortunately, the timing was never right for her to wait on him.

Around eight each night, he wished her sweet dreams, always from the road. His clients were keeping him hopping, which was great for business but inconvenient timing. How could she expect to figure out what she wanted from him if she never saw him?

Beginning with their adventures on the Fourth of July, he'd delivered swaths of vivid color to her life. After Boston, she'd needed that. Mark had plunged her into a world of black and white. She hadn't anticipated such an explosive attraction, but she'd deal with it, one way or another.

On Wednesday night, she kept her phone with her as she got ready for bed. No text. Strange, considering he'd established a pattern, but if he was in the middle of helping a client with an emergency, he wouldn't take time to text her. She'd look for one early the next morning.

But when she woke up, there was no text waiting for her. His truck wasn't in its space, either. By noon she'd begun to worry. She considered calling Roxanne to see if she'd heard anything, but she wasn't sure what she'd say if Roxanne started asking questions.

The day dragged by, the minute hand barely moving on the clock in the bakery despite a steady flow of customers. Every time the door opened, she'd look up, hoping it would be Wes. It wasn't.

She'd still heard nothing by her bedtime. No point in even bothering to lie down. She was too agitated to sleep. Instead, she left her door open, curled up on the couch, and listened for his boots on the stairs. It was almost nine when the slow, methodical sound told her he was home. And potentially exhausted, judging from his pace.

She was still dressed in the shorts and t-shirt she'd put on after work. Hurrying out the door barefoot, she met him as he topped the stairs.

His eyes widened. "Hey, Ingrid. I didn't expect—"

"Are you okay?" Her heart thumped in her chest.

He nodded. "Yeah. Just tired." He rubbed his chin, where the shadow of a beard darkened his skin. "Sorry I didn't text you."

She brushed the comment aside. He looked like hell. "Have you eaten?"

"No, but I'll..." He seemed to be searching for the words. "I'll be fine."

"I have leftovers. I'll bring them down."

"Hey, thanks, but it must be late. You should get some sleep."

"Right now, you need food more than I need sleep. I'll be over in a few minutes." Turning, she ran down the hall to her apartment. He probably needed sleep, too, but she couldn't help with that. What she could do was prepare a hearty pick-me-up meal and make sure he got some of it down before he collapsed.

14

Ingrid's unexpected appearance at the top of the stairs had been Wes's version of an oasis in the desert. And a warm meal would provide the comfort he craved.

By the time she stepped into his apartment, he'd ditched his hat and his filthy boots and was scrubbing up at the kitchen sink. His shirt was untucked and he'd rolled up his sleeves past his elbows.

If she hadn't brought him food, he would have stripped down and climbed in the shower. Instead, he grabbed a kitchen towel to mop his face and dry his hands.

"I have a pot of chili, cornbread and a six-pack of the beer you like."

"Sounds great." He lowered the towel and gazed at her standing there with her golden hair loose around her shoulders and her arms full. "How do you know what beer I like?"

"It's the kind you brought the other night."

"Do you like it?"

"Not especially."

"Then why—"

"I decided to stock some in, just in case."

"Thank you." There might be some subtext there but he wasn't up to deciphering it. He flipped the towel onto his shoulder. "Let me help you with all that."

She handed him the six-pack. "Maybe you should start with a beer while I warm up the chili and the cornbread."

"I can warm it up. If you don't mind leaving everything, you could go back to your apartment. It's way past your bedtime and—"

"Wes." She set down the food and propped her hands on her hips. "Please sit down and open a beer. I'll warm your dinner and serve it to you. No offense, but you don't look like you're up to operating a stove right now."

He sighed. "Excellent observation." Pulling out a kitchen chair, he lowered himself into it. Then he twisted off the cap on the beer and took a slow sip. "Damn, that tastes good. Thank you, Ingrid."

"You're welcome." She put the pot of chili on the stove to heat and turned on the oven before sticking the cornbread inside. "Judging from how red your eyes are, I'm going to guess I've had more sleep in the past twenty-four hours than you have."

"That's for sure." Something in her comment filtered into his brain. "Hey, did I worry you? I meant to text you, but I didn't anticipate..."

She turned toward him, her expression troubled, her voice subdued. "Did you lose a horse?"

"Almost."

"Oh, Wes."

He sucked in air and blew it out. The tension hadn't dissipated, might not for a while. He took another sip of the beer. "My client called me out last night around seven. Colic."

"Oh, dear."

"At first it seemed manageable. We walked her around and she seemed to be doing better. We were in a watch-and-see situation. Monitored her during the night and everything looked good. Then about four in the morning, it all went south."

He scrubbed a hand over his face as if to wipe away the memory of the woman's panic when she realized her mare might die. Roxanne had looked like that the day they'd lost Scooter.

"You don't have to talk about it if you don't want to."

He glanced up at her. "I probably should. I had a vet tell me that locking it away inside is a sure way to burn out." He hesitated. "On the other hand, I don't have to dump the story on you. I can spill the beans to Dad or Pete next time I see one of them."

Her gaze softened. "I'd prefer it if you told me."

How could he refuse such a heartfelt request? "It was like going through the nightmare with Scooter all over again. At least this time the ending was different."

"Was that because you'd been through it before?"

"Maybe." He took another sip of his beer. "That's something to hold onto. I might have recognized a tad earlier that we had to get that mare into surgery. Scooter died on the way to the clinic. The mare didn't, but it was the longest sixty miles I've ever driven."

"You drove?"

"Had to. That poor woman was in no condition to take the wheel. She spent most of the trip sobbing."

"And neither of you had slept."

"That's right."

"She didn't have anybody else around to help with this? A husband? Siblings? One of her friends?"

"No. She's elderly and her husband died last year. They don't have kids. No relatives close by and she hasn't lived in town long. This mare is her whole world."

"And you saved her. Saved them both, really."

"Yeah. We stayed until the mare was out of danger. Then I drove her home. She didn't want me to leave."

"Not surprising, after what you'd both been through."

"She wanted to feed me, but I just...I had to get some distance." His head felt like it was stuffed with wool that was crammed in so tight it put pressure behind his eyes. They kept watering. He took the towel off his shoulder and mopped his face again. "I'm really sorry I didn't text you while that was going on, but—"

"I understand." Her voice was a caress.

Glancing up, he met her gaze. He saw compassion in her blue eyes, but something else that made his heart rate pick up.

She turned back to the stove before he could figure out what it meant.

He cleared his throat. "I'm guessing the chili's warmed up."

"It is." She twisted the knobs on the stove, shutting off the heat.

"If you want to head off to bed, I can take it from here."

"I don't think I can do that." She faced him. "You've been through the wringer. More than anything, I think you need someone to hold you."

His heart started pounding like crazy. "Ingrid, I'm—"

"Just let me hold you, Wes."

His breath caught. Could he handle that? Even as exhausted as he was, he could be playing with fire if he allowed her that close. But yearning swamped him. He swallowed. "I'd like that."

She smiled. "Then the chili can wait." Walking toward him, she held out her hand.

His skin prickled and his ears buzzed. Taking her incredibly soft hand, he stood. Upright now. A little dizzy and disoriented, but upright.

She led him down the hall, her grip firm. He wouldn't have resisted under normal circumstances, but certainly not after twenty-four hours of living hell. He desperately wanted...he wasn't even sure. He'd trust her to figure it out.

His bedroom was dark and she made no attempt to change that. Stopping beside his bed, she cradled his face in both hands.

"I need a shave."

"No, you don't. You need me." She brushed her full lips over his mouth.

Resting his hands on her hips, he closed his aching eyes and abandoned himself to the experience of being slowly, lovingly kissed by Ingrid.

She caressed his unshaven jaw and paid homage to his mouth. The aroma of baked goods mingled with her lemon shampoo, surrounding him with the scent he'd grown to crave.

The gentle, undemanding pressure of her lips soothed him. As the tension gradually drained from his tight muscles, he wrapped her loosely in his arms with a sigh of relief.

She leaned back and glanced up at him. Light from the hallway caught the soft glow in her eyes. "Better?"

"Getting there." He had a million questions but he wouldn't ask them. Not now.

"Good." Her gaze held his as she unbuttoned his shirt with deliberate care. When she had it undone, she slid her hands up his chest.

Her touch was magic. He closed his eyes, drew in a slow breath and let it out. "Please do that some more."

"Like this?" She stroked him again.

"Mm."

"And this?" She began a slow massage.

He groaned softly. "Yeah. Where did you—"

"I knead bread for a living."

"Never thought...of that." Behind his fly, his cock was waking up.

"Kneading bread builds strong fingers." Her warm breath tickled his chest a moment before her mouth made contact with his skin in a moist, erotic kiss.

He gasped and a wave of heat went straight to his crotch.

She pulled back. "Too much?"

"God, no. But I'm getting—"

"Is that a problem?"

He stared at her. "Not for me." But he hadn't expected her to—

She gave him a Cheshire Cat smile before returning to licking and kissing his chest, pushing his shirt over his shoulders and down his arms until it fell to the floor. Then she undid the metal button on his jeans.

Evidently his cock finally got the message and surged to life. Lack of sleep didn't factor in. When she unzipped his fly, he was wide awake. All over.

Cupping her face in one hand and wrapping his arm around her waist, he lifted her into a kiss far steamier than hers had been. He was as careful as humanly possible about his beard, but he was hungry for her sweet lips.

When she reached inside his jeans, he thrust his tongue deep into her mouth. Her magic hands caused havoc with whatever control he had left and he had to let her go so he could back away and drag in air. "I think...we've reached the point...of no return."

"I think you're right." She whipped her t-shirt over her head and dropped it.

He'd started to shove his jeans and briefs down when she reached behind her back and unhooked her bra. He paused in mid-motion and quietly cursed the dim light.

Yet enough filtered in to give him a stunning visual of her plump breasts in sepia tones. They quivered invitingly when she wiggled out of her shorts and panties. He looked his fill, memorizing each luscious curve.

"Do you need help?" Her voice rippled with laughter.

"I need whatever you're willing to give me." He shucked his jeans.

15

Breathe, girl. After meeting Wes in the hall after his shower last week, Ingrid should have been prepared for her first glimpse of him without the towel. So much for that theory.

The dim light could be a blessing. Gazing upon his muscled body and his jutting, impressive erection when he was partially hidden in shadows had given her what used to be called the vapors. A fully illuminated Wes might cause her to faint dead away.

After tossing back the covers on the bed, he turned and gave her a long look. "Second thoughts?"

"No thoughts at all. My brain checked out when you took off your jeans."

"Then we're in the same boat." He closed the distance and pulled her into his arms, maneuvering her onto the bed and climbing in beside her.

She tingled with anticipation. All that male beauty and heat she'd been contemplating for days was finally within reach. She laid a hand on his lightly furred chest, right over his rapidly beating heart. "Feeling better?"

"You have no idea."

"Then let's take it up a notch."

"Yes, ma'am." He coaxed her to her back and began a leisurely exploration of her body that soon had her writhing beneath him.

When he returned from his journey to visit her mouth, she interrupted the kiss. "I didn't mean...me. This is...supposed to be...about you."

His smile was pure sin. "It is about me. I'm worshipping your body."

"But you need—"

"I'm getting exactly what I need." And he kissed his way back to her breasts to worship them some more.

He did a fabulous job, too. Too fabulous, actually. He was pushing her to the brink, and she craved all he had to give. But there was an important item she hadn't factored into the equation. "Do you have condoms?"

He lifted his head, gazing up at her through his lashes. "Yes."

Thank goodness. "Are you planning to *use* one of those condoms anytime soon?"

Evidently he found that funny, because he was laughing as he reached into the bedside table drawer. "I'd be delighted to." He kissed her forehead, her nose and her mouth before leaning back so he could suit up. "But just so you know, that'll be game over." He moved between her thighs. "I've delayed on purpose." He probed her entrance.

Her breath caught. "I suspected."

"Now that you're here, I don't want this to be over." He slid only the tip of his cock inside.

She closed her eyes, savoring the sensations he was creating. "Me, either."

"I want to remember every moment of this night." He eased in a little deeper.

"So do I."

"Good." He took a deep breath. "Remember this." And he plunged deep.

She gasped and clutched his hips, holding him there.

He put his lips close to her ear. "Perfect."

Her response drifted on a sigh of pleasure. "Yes."

Drawing back, he shoved home again. "Simple."

"Uh-huh." Tiny fires ignited along the path of exquisite friction he created.

"Elegant." His warm breath bathed her sensitive ear canal as he stroked again, and again, creating a tantalizing rhythm that tightened the inner coil poised to give her a climax.

"Powerful." He moved faster, drove deeper. Tucking his big hands under her hips, he lifted her higher, changing the angle, intensifying the pleasure of each thrust.

Her climax arrived, blasting through her like a freight train, tearing cries of joyful release from her throat until she was hoarse and gasping for air.

"*Yes!*" His bellow of triumph followed soon after as he pushed home and pulsed within her, his big body shuddering, his ragged breathing drowning out her cries.

Slick with sweat, she clung to him as her world spun and gradually slowed. Eyes closed, she worked to steady her breathing.

He nestled his cheek against her shoulder. "So great."

"I know." Better than her wildest dreams, and she'd had some whoppers.

To her amazement, he roused himself long enough to dispose of the condom, whereas she was so blissed out she could barely move.

Then he came back to bed and gathered her close. "Don't let me fall asleep."

Making love to Wes and enjoying the most amazing orgasm of her life must have altered her brain chemistry because she considered that a reasonable request. "Sure. Okay."

"Thanks." He gave her a sweet kiss and settled back with a sigh.

She closed her eyes, savoring the warmth of his body cradling hers.

* * *

The room was still dark when she woke. After a moment of confusion, she oriented herself—Wes's apartment, Wes's bed, Wes, stretched out beside her with his arm around her waist. She'd agreed not to let him fall asleep. That had certainly worked out well.

No telling how many hours had passed, but she'd better find out. Sliding out of bed without disturbing Wes was easy. Quite likely he wouldn't wake up unless the ENHS marching band came through playing *Stars and Stripes Forever*.

She gathered her clothes and took them into the kitchen where the light was still on. Wes's phone sat on the counter and she checked the time. Three on the dot. Her internal alarm had worked perfectly.

The six-pack of beer sat warming on his kitchen table. He'd had only a few sips of the one he'd opened, but it would be flat by now. After throwing on her clothes, she poured out the beer and put the bottle in his recycling bin. Then she stuck the pot of chili and the cornbread in the fridge, along with the rest of the beer.

No telling how long Wes would sleep. Or whether he had appointments this morning. As conscientious as he was, he'd probably set an alert on his phone if he did have to be somewhere.

Picking up the phone, she walked back to his bedroom and laid it on his nightstand. He didn't stir.

Back in the kitchen she located a scrap of paper and a pen.

Dear Wes,
It's three o'clock and I'm heading back to my place. I've put the chili, the beer and the cornbread in your fridge. When you surface, if you have time, text me. I had a wonderful time.
Ingrid

A wonderful time, indeed. As a bonus, she'd helped pull him out of the psychically draining place he'd fallen into. He was a talented practitioner with empathy for the struggles of his clients and patients.

He might consider that a flaw, but she wouldn't change a thing. Over time he'd learn how to handle the resulting stress. Considering his amazing family and his own natural resilience, he'd be fine.

After turning off the light in the kitchen, she left his apartment and walked back to her own. She didn't want to leave him. They'd made love but they hadn't talked afterward. The experience felt warm, cozy and...incomplete.

If his work schedule continued to be crazy, they might not have a chance to be together again any time soon. Unless he created an opportunity. After what they'd shared, he just might.

Funny how the hallway changed dimensions depended on how she was feeling about Wes. When she'd been afraid that their relationship was becoming too intimate, the hallway had seemed dangerously short. But after tonight, when she'd been as close to him as she'd ever been to another human being, the hallway seemed to stretch for miles.

16

Wes woke to the sound of his phone alarm and rolled over to silence it. Only it wasn't on the nightstand where he always put it. It was on the other nightstand. Still groggy, he sat up and rubbed his eyes. Why would he have...oh, yeah. Ingrid must have brought it in.

He glanced around the room as if she'd somehow materialize. Naturally she wouldn't because sunlight streamed in his bedroom window and tempting bakery smells drifted from downstairs. She was working.

While he'd been sawing logs, she'd already spent several hours involved in a demanding job after losing sleep because of him. She'd also chosen to make love to him. Imagine that.

Flopping back onto the pillow he stared at the ceiling and allowed the wonder of last night to flood through him. When he'd left her on Sunday he'd figured there was only a fifty-fifty chance such a thing would ever happen. He'd spent a fair amount of time cursing her ex for making her so gun-shy.

Then he'd heard nothing for days other than her brief replies to his texts. She hadn't initiated any texts to him, so he'd figured his chances were dwindling.

To be fair, he hadn't been around much, especially the past day and a half. And she was the kind of person who would deliver her response, yay or nay, in person.

Well, she'd done that last night. Miracle of miracles, she'd taken the plunge. He might have convinced himself he'd dreamed the whole thing, except the scent of lemons and pastries clung to his sheets.

Climbing out of bed, he wandered into the kitchen and read the note she'd left. *I had a wonderful time.* His body warmed. She'd mentioned texting when he was awake, but he craved the sight of her, even if they couldn't talk while she was working.

His first appointment wasn't until eleven. He'd moved a couple of them to next week when he'd figured out the colic situation was dire. Then he'd neglected to reset his alarm, which meant he had plenty of time to spare for a change.

Before he went downstairs, though, he needed a shower, a shave, and something to eat besides pastries. Even his iron stomach wouldn't be able to handle coffee and a bear claw when he hadn't eaten real food since...yikes, night before last. No wonder he was spacey.

After a nice long shower and a careful shave, he had chili and cornbread for breakfast while he checked on the mare's post-op progress and talked briefly with his client. The mare was doing fine and his client sounded much better today.

With forty minutes to spare before he had to leave for his appointment, he was ready to mosey down to Pie in the Sky. He picked up his hat on his way out of the apartment and started down the stairs.

Ingrid came through the door carrying a white bakery box. Clearly startled, she paused and looked up at him. "Hi! On your way to an appointment?" She sounded out of breath and her cheeks were pink.

His breathing wasn't all that steady, either. She looked great. "On my way to see you."

"I'm on a break."

"How long of a break?"

"Twenty minutes. I was just going to…never mind. This is perfect, running into each other. We need to talk."

"All right. Do you want—"

"I'll come up. This is for you, anyway."

"You brought me pastries?" Life just got better and better.

"I did."

"Thank you." *I don't need them, though. Just let me kiss you and hold you and I'll be on a contact high all day.* He backed up the stairs and waited for her on the landing.

"I wasn't sure if you were awake yet since you hadn't texted."

"I decided to get cleaned up and just come down."

"Now you won't need to. We only had one more chocolate éclair in the case. I decided to snag it, plus a couple of bear claws and a cheese Danish." She reached the landing and handed him the box.

"Wow, thank you. All my favorites." Except now he was holding a bakery box instead of Ingrid. "We can go into my apartment. It's closer."

"That's okay. I was hoping we'd have a chance to talk, but we can do it here." She was breathing fast.

"We can, but wouldn't you rather—"

"Not really. I mean, if we go into your apartment, then..."

"What? I'm not going to try and seduce you on your twenty-minute break."

"I know." She glanced toward the stairway. "But I don't want Abigail to suspect anything."

"Does she know you were bringing these to me?"

"I didn't specify what I was going to do with them."

"Ah." He was getting the picture. "You want to keep this on the down-low."

"Under the circumstances, I think that's a good idea."

"What circumstances?"

"For starters, we're neighbors."

"Yes, ma'am. Last time I checked, that was still the case."

"It's not like I didn't think of that before, but I hadn't considered all the implications."

"Such as?"

"Abigail still has her apartment here, too. She wasn't here last night, thank goodness, but what if she had been? She might have heard us."

"Would that be so terrible?"

"No. Yes. I don't know." She glanced at the stairway again. "I never expected to have sex with the man who lives down the hall from my apartment and over the bakery where I work. It makes this...complicated."

He hadn't considered how that might impact her day-to-day life, except in positive ways. Apparently she was concerned about negative ones. "It doesn't have to be complicated."

"It already is."

"Do you regret what happened last night?" He didn't really want to hear the answer, but he had to know.

Her brow furrowed. "No. Please don't think that. It's just—" She blew out a breath. "I'm making a mess of this."

He shifted the pastry box to one hand and cupped her chin in the other. "No, you're not. It's fine. Whatever you need, that's what we'll do."

Some of the sparkle returned to her eyes. "Yeah?"

"Yeah." He yearned to kiss her, but he couldn't without dumping the bakery box. He loved that she'd brought him pastries but the box was seriously cramping his style. "Are you available tonight? If you don't want Abigail to know we'll be together, then we can—"

"She already mentioned she'll be at Luke's the next two nights."

Lady Luck was smiling on him. "Are you free, then?"

Excitement flashed in her eyes. "I am, but what about you?"

The box had to go. He set it on the floor and nudged back his hat. "I'm all yours. I'll put the out of office message on my phone alerting my clients before I go to my next appointment."

"Oh." She licked her lips.

His groin tightened in response.

"What time did you want to get together?"

His heart rate jacked up as the possibilities expanded. "I was thinking from about six until..." Oh, hell. Might as well go for broke. "Actually, I want to spend the entire night with you. But we'll sleep, I promise. I don't want to mess up your—"

"Yes." She sounded breathless. "My place, then?"

"Sure. I'll bring pizza."

"Pizza would be great."

"Then I'll be there at six."

"Make it five-thirty."

"Even better." He took a step toward her.

She backed up.

He halted. "Hey, I'm not going to pounce. I just—"

"It's not you. It's me." She swallowed. "I'm afraid I might grab you."

And boy, did that turn up his thermostat. He'd said he wouldn't pounce, so he shoved his hands in his pockets. "You're welcome to grab me anytime, anywhere." It didn't come out as casually as he would have liked.

"I'll remember that. I'd better get downstairs."

He checked his phone. "You still have a little time."

"Not much." She turned to leave. Then she spun back and clutched his face in both hands. "Consider yourself grabbed." She kissed him hard on the mouth, let him go and started toward the stairs.

He caught her by the arm before she'd taken two steps. Pulling her in tight, he lowered his head. "My turn."

She melted into his arms with a sigh that stirred his blood and made his jeans pinch. Last night he'd been nearly catatonic from stress and exhaustion, and her kiss had brought him back to the land of the living.

This morning he was awake, from the crown of his hat to the sole of his boots. He intended to savor the intense pleasure of exploring her mouth. Sure enough, it was more delicious than any pastry in the box at his feet. He couldn't get enough.

No telling how long he would have kept on kissing her, but eventually she pressed her palms against his chest and put some distance between them. He groaned in protest.

"I have to go."

He gazed into blue eyes hot with passion. "We'll continue this tonight."

"I suspect we will."

"Count on it."

"Now I really have to go." She wiggled free and backed away. "Do I look kissed?"

"You do to me, but I'm the guy who was just kissing you." And he couldn't wait to repeat the pleasure.

She took a deep breath and let it out slowly. "I can do this." She smoothed a hand over her hair before starting toward the stairs. She paused with one hand on the railing. "Oh, and Wes?"

"Yeah?"

"Don't forget the other item. The one from your nightstand."

With that parting shot she disappeared down the stairs, leaving him standing like a department store mannequin.

It took a few minutes to get a rein on the lust she'd just mainlined into his veins. Once he had his body back under some semblance of control, he pulled out his phone and recorded his out of office message. It sounded a little guttural, but that couldn't be helped. He glanced at the time before he slipped the phone in his pocket.

Six hours, forty-five minutes and counting.

17

After work, as Ingrid straightened the apartment and put fresh sheets on the bed, anticipation revved her up more than one of her Firecracker lattes. Last night Wes had been wiped out by his ordeal. This time he'd be rested. She couldn't wait for five-thirty.

She stood in front of the fish poster. "Okay, fish, what's your take on this? Are you up for bike-riding lessons? Or is this an incredibly stupid move on my part?"

The fish didn't answer, but somebody rapped sharply on her doorframe. She walked to the partially open door and flung it open.

Wes stood there in all his cowboy glory, a pizza box in one hand and a bottle of red wine in the other.

His smile tugged at her heart. "I would have come riding up to your door mounted on a white horse and wearing a white hat, but it's tough to get those on short notice."

"Come in, you crazy cowboy. That's a huge pizza. You must be hungry."

"Oh, I am."

I hope you're hungry because I'm not a fan of leftover pizza."

"One more thing we have in common."

"You're making that up. Most guys I've known are fine with day-old pizza."

"I'm not most guys."

"That's becoming abundantly clear." She glanced at him. "Do you want to eat in the living room or in the—"

"Don't care." He put down the pizza and the wine on the coffee table. Then he laid his hat brim-side up on the box before walking toward her. Heat flared in the depths of his eyes.

Heart pounding, she held his gaze. There was no mistaking his intentions. "What about the pizza?"

"I don't give a damn about food right now. I'm hungry for you." Closing the distance between them, he scooped her into his arms and carried her down the hall, just like he had during the three-legged race. Crossing the finish line tonight would be even more fun.

He undressed her with tender care and lingering kisses before tossing back the covers and lifting her onto the smooth sheets. She lay in the glow from the setting sun while he unsnapped his cuffs and started in on the row running down the front of this shirt.

He maintained eye contact as he took off his shirt and leaned against her dresser to pull off his boots. That constant connection fired her up like one of her baking ovens.

Before he took off his jeans, he reached in his pocket, took out a condom and laid it on the bedside table. That was caring. And sexy.

Although she'd enjoyed the last unveiling of his aroused cock, the thrill this time was even stronger. If anything, she was even more eager because she'd experienced the effects it produced. Last night he'd been focused on exploring her body, but considering his declaration, he wouldn't delay the moment she craved.

He wasted no time taking off his jeans and briefs. She tightened her jaw to hold back a whimper of longing. Fishes and bicycles be damned. She was gonna teach that fish to ride.

He rolled on the condom with as little fuss as he'd taken with undressing. Although he could be a tease and a jokester, the rich vein of passion that ran though him clearly outweighed every other impulse. Judging from the fire in his eyes, he'd tapped into it now.

He continued to focus on her eyes as he climbed into bed and settled between her thighs. Clutching his bare shoulders gave her a jolt of pleasure.

No wonder she'd fought the urge to grab him earlier today. And lost the fight. Fully clothed or naked, it didn't matter. She just wanted to get her hands on him. His muscled body begged to be kneaded and massaged.

Moving with unerring confidence, he nudged her slick channel once with the tip of his cock as if finding his place. Then, his gaze never leaving hers, he thrust deep.

She made a low sound of satisfaction deep in her throat.

He smiled. "Better?"

Her heart beat a happy tattoo. He'd repeated the one-word question she'd asked last night. She replied with his answer. "Getting there."

"Good."

Ah, she loved that he'd filed last night's words away, even when he'd been battling sleep deprivation and stress. It told her how much making love to her mattered to him. And how much it mattered to her.

Then he began to move with an easy rhythm. Yet their intimate connection had such heat and power that her body clenched, anticipating the tight spiral of need and the explosive release.

Pumping slowly, he rested his weight on his forearms and lowered his body so that his lightly furred chest brushed lazily over her erect nipples. He brought his body heat with him, surrounding her in a sensual cocoon of warmth and erotic friction.

And through it all, his gaze remained focused on hers—steady, sure, glowing with joy. As the pressure mounted, she drew him close and gathered strength from his solid presence and the unwavering light in his eyes.

As the first tremor rippled through her core, his mouth tilted in a soft smile. He continued to stroke in an easy, unhurried way as she gradually, inevitably, surrendered to the undulating, whirling glory of release. Gasping his name, she arched beneath him.

Only then did he increase the pace. The flame burned brighter in his dark eyes as his rapid thrusts swept her toward a second climax. Driving deep, he broke eye contact at last, throwing back his head and claiming his release with a wild cry of triumph.

Happiness spread through her like warm syrup, filling every nook and cranny.

Still breathing fast, he lowered his gaze. "You're smiling."

"So are you."

"Damn straight. You give me so much to smile about it's not funny."

She reached up and stroked his freshly shaven cheek. "You make me smile, too. Especially when we're like this."

He grinned. "Then we'll have to spend more time this way, won't we?"

* * *

"While I wouldn't change a thing, this order of events has one obvious disadvantage." Wes buttoned his jeans. He'd taken his cue from Ingrid. Since she'd started putting on her clothes, he would, too. "How do you feel about cold pizza?"

"I like it better hot."

"Me, too." He waggled his eyebrows at her as he grabbed his shirt and shoved his arms into the sleeves.

She smiled. "Could you do me a favor?"

"Anything."

"Leave your shirt unsnapped."

He glanced at her bare breasts and the bra she held in her hand. "Could you do me a favor?"

She looked a little wary. "Like what?"

"Go braless."

"Braless? Not topless?"

"A t-shirt and no bra is more subtle than topless. I like subtle."

"Done." She tossed the bra aside and pulled her t-shirt over her head. "How's that?"

His breath caught. It was happening again, another moment when he became so entranced by her he couldn't move. "Hold still."

"Why? Is something wrong?"

"No." He sounded hoarse. "Something's right." The last rays of the setting sun poured golden light through her bedroom window, caressing her tousled hair, her flushed cheeks and the soft t-shirt draped over her breasts. She was so beautiful it made his throat hurt.

"Can I move yet?" She sounded amused.

He took a deep breath. "Sure. Absolutely."

"You're good for a girl's ego." She walked toward him. "I don't think I've ever dazzled a man before."

"You're dazzling one, now." He pulled her into his arms. "It's happened to me twice, once on Sunday and just now. I'm going along minding my own business and whap, your beauty hits me upside the head. I can't stop looking at you."

"Sunday? You weren't distracted by work when I caught you staring?"

"Nope. Dazzled by you."

She smiled. "Which makes me feel like some legendary beauty like Cleopatra or Helen of Troy. Who wouldn't enjoy that?"

"Then it's win-win." He gazed into her sea-blue eyes. "If I start kissing you again, the cheese on the pizza will have congealed."

"We don't want congealed cheese."

"No." He drifted closer to her inviting lips. "But I could order another—"

"That's not happening." She placed her hand over his mouth. "We're eating this one before the cheese congeals." Easing away from him, she headed toward the door. "I'm hungry."

"Me, too. For everything." He followed her into the living room where the pizza and wine sat on the coffee table. "Do you want to eat it here or—"

"I vote for the kitchen. There's no good reason to juggle plates unless we're going to watch TV. I won't speak for you, but I'm not in the mood for that."

"I'd rather watch you."

She laughed. "Ditto." She picked up the wine. "Hey, this is the kind that Rox discovered."

"I remembered seeing a bottle like that in her apartment when I was here in March." He carried the pizza into the kitchen and put it on the table. "I took a chance you liked it, too."

"Oh, yeah. It became our go-to for girls' night. We like the wine and the screw-top convenience." She placed it next to the pizza box. "Whatever kind you got smells amazing." She pulled two plates from the cupboard and handed them to him along with a couple of napkins. "And familiar."

"It should."

"Did you get a veggie one?" She brought wine glasses over.

"Yes, ma'am." Opening the wine, he poured them each a glass.

"Awesome." She lifted the lid and peered inside. "Mm, my favorite." She glanced up. "That's not a coincidence, is it?"

"Nope. I'm really beginning to appreciate the benefits of living in a small town. I asked what you usually ordered and they could tell me."

"Aw. Thank you. What a sweet gesture."

"You're welcome."

"Just out of curiosity, what's your favorite?"

"I'm more of a pepperoni and sausage man, but I like everything so this'll be great." And he'd eat veggie pizza forever if she'd keep looking at him like that.

"Then next time we'll get half veggies and half pepperoni and sausage."

"Boy do I love hearing that."

"See, you're making a sacrifice by eating—"

"The pizza's fine. I'm talking about the fact that you're already planning for next time."

"Oh." She paused and smiled at him. "I did just say that, didn't I?"

"Uh-huh." He picked up both wine glasses and gave her one. "To another pizza night."

"I'll drink to that." She touched her glass to his and held his gaze as she took a sip.

He rejoiced in the glow of excitement in her eyes. For two cents, he'd postpone this meal. They could always—

"We should eat our pizza." Her voice was a little husky.

"Or we could forget about this pizza and order another one."

"No." She put down her glass and took her seat. "We're eating the one that you so generously brought over. On top of that you made sure it was my favorite. That's special." She opened the box and took out a slice.

"What's special is that you agreed to spend tonight with me." He took his seat and helped himself to pizza.

"I wanted to. And it works out well since Abigail and Luke are out at his house tonight."

"And tomorrow night."

"You want to do this again tomorrow night?"

"Sure, if I don't get any calls." He sighed. "Much as I'd like to forward my calls tomorrow night, or any night you're available, I can't abandon my clients like that."

"And you shouldn't. Spending two nights in a row together probably wouldn't be wise, anyway."

"You mean because you'd lose sleep? I promise that I'll make sure you don't."

"And I believe you." She gave him a fond glance. "It's just that the more often we spend the night together, the more likely someone will find out. I'd like to avoid that complication, at least for now." She finished her slice of pizza and took another one out of the box.

Her mention of the complication issue had bothered him when she'd brought it up this morning. He didn't like it any better now. Hiding a relationship seemed way more complicated than making it public. "How long do you want to keep this under wraps?"

"I don't know." She chewed and swallowed. "Until we figure some things out, I guess."

Until *she* figured some things out, apparently. He knew exactly what he wanted.

She gazed at him. "You don't seem happy with the idea."

"I'm not very good at keeping secrets." Especially when he wanted to shout the truth to the rooftops.

She frowned. "Is that going to be a problem?"

The wariness was back in her eyes. And he'd put it there by pushing. "No, it's fine." He needed to be patient. She was already giving him way more than he'd expected. Getting greedy would drive a wedge between them. No way was he going to do that. "You're right. It's a lot of new." Especially for her. She was the one healing from a bad breakup.

"Thanks, Wes."

"For what?"

"For understanding."

And didn't that make him feel all warm and fuzzy.

"The pizza's delicious, by the way." She took another bite. "It didn't get *that* cold."

"It helps that it's July and not December."

She laughed. "That's for sure. The delivery guys use those insulated carriers, but still. We'd usually end up sticking it back in the oven for a little while."

He polished off another slice of pizza. "It sounds like the three of you had a good time when you all lived up here."

"Oh, we did, but I can guarantee Abigail and Rox are thrilled with the direction their lives have taken."

And hopefully one day soon, Ingrid would feel the same way about the direction her life was going. "Do you still get together?"

"Once in a while. It's a little trickier to coordinate, now."

"True."

"But I'm enjoying spending time with my new neighbor." Her foot caressed his calf under the table and he jumped.

"You don't say?" His words came out slightly garbled as her foot moved higher.

"Mm."

His breathing quickened. "Like now."

"Uh-huh." She smiled. "I'm thinking the meal's over."

"Me, too." He stood and held out his hand. "Time for dessert." He'd leave the complication issue alone for now. If they made wonderful love to each other enough times, the problem might take care of itself.

18

True to his word, Wes made sweet love to her and then insisted they were going to sleep. She was convinced that wouldn't work. Tucked into the curve of his virile body, she resigned herself to lying awake all night in a state of sexual frustration. Two minutes later she was asleep.

A minute after that, or so it seemed, he kissed her awake. "Time to leave your cozy bed, Sleeping Beauty."

The rumble of his deep voice in the dark bedroom roused her in more ways than one. She snuggled against him. "Did my alarm go off?"

"I set mine on vibrate for a couple minutes earlier." He nibbled on her lip. "I wanted to wake you up myself. I cancelled yours just now."

She wound her arms around his neck. "Very nice, except now I don't want to get up."

"What time do you need to be downstairs?"

"I like to get there about quarter-to-four."

"You need forty-five minutes to get ready?"

She smiled at the disbelief in his voice. "I do if I don't want to rush."

"Then you'd better climb out of this bed."

"What if I don't want to?" She stroked her hand down his hard body and discovered he was as awake as she was.

"Then you'll have to rush."

"You're good at that." She grasped his firm cock. "Any tips?"

"Sorry, I'm all out of tips. You just short-circuited my brain."

"Your brain is located down there?"

"More times than I care to admit."

"Got another condom?"

"Yes, ma'am."

"Let's put it to use. Then you can teach me how to rush."

"Yes, ma'am." He suited up in no time and found easy entry into her slick channel. Then he slid his hands under her bottom and put his mouth close to her ear. "We don't have time to fool around. You're going to come, and come fast, so hang on tight."

Heart pounding, she wrapped her arms around him. "I'm strapped in. Let 'er rip."

His first thrust lifted her off the mattress.

She gasped and shivered in delight as he followed up with rapid strokes that soon had her panting and hanging on for dear life. He took her on a wild thrill ride that had her yelling as if she'd claimed the front seat of the most daring roller coaster in the park. Her climax arrived in a burst of fireworks.

He followed right on her heels, his breathless laughter filling the room. Braced above her, he gave a little whoop of joy. "Damn, that was fun!"

"Sure...was." She gulped for air.

"You okay?"

"Oh, yeah." Although her heart pounded and she was struggling for breath, she'd had the time of her life. She hadn't considered that Wes was a former athlete who'd recently been pumping iron. He'd brought his A-game just now and the results had been spectacular. "Let's do that again sometime."

He put his mouth next to her ear. "My pleasure."

* * *

Despite Wes's help or maybe because of it, Ingrid arrived at Pie in the Sky about five minutes later than usual. Abigail was already there prepping for the first round of baking. Acting normal after a hot goodbye kiss a few moments ago took some acting skills.

She'd put on her lipstick *after* that kiss and straightened her clothes, but adrenaline course through her veins. Fortunately, they had a lot to do and Abigail didn't seem to notice anything unusual. The Guzzling Grizzly had emailed a large pie order and if they filled it today they wouldn't have to work on Sunday.

When Abigail mentioned that Ingrid looked happy, her response was easy. "I got a really good night's sleep."

Very true, although hard to believe. Evidently great lovemaking and Wes's body curled around hers had combined to give her seven hours of deep and restorative rest.

Add to that a vigorous quickie session this morning, and she had more energy than she'd had in weeks. They'd made tentative plans to see each other tonight, assuming a client didn't contact him with an emergency.

She congratulated herself on working side-by-side with Abigail and chatting about plans for the weekend like nothing unusual was going on. She even mentioned she and Wes might go riding.

Abigail seemed to take it all at face value. Then, minutes before their two employees were due to arrive, Abigail paused to give her a no-nonsense, direct stare.

She stared right back. Good friends could get away with that. "What?"

"I'm trying to figure out what's different about you. Did you dye your hair?"

"No."

"Did you adopt a kitten?"

"No. I would have told you."

"Not if you wanted to surprise me."

"No kitten."

"Did you win a small jackpot? I know it's not the Powerball. You couldn't keep that a secret, but—"

"I didn't hit the jackpot." She smiled because in a way, she had. "Like I said, I got a great night's sleep. That can do wonders."

"Granted, but you've slept well other nights. There's more to it than that. Are you and Luke planning something special for my birthday?"

"Um..." She'd meant to talk to Luke about birthday plans for Abigail but hadn't done it yet. She needed to, though. It was coming up next month.

"Hey, if that's what's going on, don't answer. I'd hate to ruin whatever you two are planning." Abigail's attention turned to the front door. "Hey, Yolanda!" She glanced back at Ingrid. "Don't tell Luke I asked about my birthday, okay?"

"I won't." Whew. If she could get through today, she wouldn't see Abigail again until Monday. By then she should be more comfortable with the new arrangement and wouldn't be giving off any *I have a secret* vibes.

In the meantime, she'd text Luke and find out if he was planning a birthday surprise. It would be the first time he'd celebrated with Abigail so he should be planning a surprise, right? If not, she'd suggest that he get on that ASAP.

Wes walked in around nine, after the morning rush. She came so close to spilling a latte down her front. His grin told her he'd noticed, too. He nudged back his hat and sauntered over to the counter.

She could have asked Doug, their other young employee, to handle Wes's coffee order. Doug was turning into an excellent barista. But when Wes gave her a quick wink, she accepted his challenge.

She cleared her throat. "What can I get for you?"

His dark eyes gleamed with mischief. "I dunno. What's good here?"

"Everything."

"Do you have a suggestion for me?"

Several. "How about a Firecracker?"

"Better not." He held her gaze and his lips twitched. "I had one earlier this morning. Nearly took the top of my head off."

Heat flooded her cheeks. *You are a devil, Wes Sawyer.* "Then maybe you need something tamer. Something you can handle."

"Good idea. That'll give my system a chance to settle down before I try something like that again."

Yowza. She cleared the lust from her throat. "Regular coffee, then?"

"Please." His voice was like velvet.

"Something from the case?"

"No, thank you. A generous lady brought me several pastries yesterday and I have some left. They're out in my truck. I'm well taken care of."

She lowered her voice. "You didn't need to come in for this coffee, did you?"

"Not for the coffee, no." The mischief in his gaze had morphed into something hotter. "How're you doing?"

"I'm doing well, thank you."

"Any issues?"

"Nothing I can't take care of."

"Glad to hear it. I—"

"Hey, brother of mine! Fancy meeting you here, stranger."

"Hey, sis!" Without missing a beat, he turned and enveloped Roxanne in a bear hug.

She smiled at Ingrid over his shoulder. "Hi, there."

Ingrid's heart thumped double-time. She hadn't expected to run into her friend this morning. Or any morning for that matter.

For reasons known only to her libido, in the past forty-eight hours she'd stopped thinking of Wes as Roxanne's brother. Which was a *major* oversight. The flush rising in her cheeks confirmed it. Thankfully her voice came out perfectly normal. "Hi. Want your usual latte?"

"You know it, girlfriend." She stepped away from Wes and patted him on the cheek. "What a bonus to get a hug from my elusive brother. Haven't seen much of you lately, big guy."

"Sorry about that. You know how it goes. Working my tail off."

Ingrid kept herself busy making Rox's latte so she had an excuse to avert her gaze.

"I know. Dad said you and Ingrid went riding last Sunday, though. That must have been fun."

"Yeah, it was."

Rox turned to her. "Isn't Wes the best trail riding buddy ever?"

Ingrid concentrated on pouring the steamed milk into the cup. If she looked up, she'd probably end up scalding herself. "He is. And I loved being on a horse again. We had a great time."

A boulder settled into Ingrid's stomach. Rox wouldn't dream that her best friend—who was only three weeks past a breakup—would sleep with her brother. Not in a million years. Even if someone flat-out told her it had happened, she wouldn't believe them. Ah, the guilt.

"I came in for my latte," Rox said. "But also to ask if you want to get together for a girls' night. Michael's working and I haven't hung out with you in a while, so I was thinking a bottle of wine, a movie, maybe a board game. Are you up for that? Say around six?"

The universe was bringing her to heel for her transgressions. She studiously avoided looking at Wes. "Sure, why not?" She hoped he wouldn't be hurt by her quick capitulation, but their plans had been tentative. He might not even be available.

She'd also have to scour the apartment and remove any sign that Wes had spent the night there. But what if she missed something?

"Great! I could bring a pizza, that veggie kind you like. You probably haven't had one in ages."

She swallowed a bubble of hysterical laughter. "I'd love that."

"Thought so." Rox turned to Wes, who'd been pretending great interest in the coffee menu posted on the wall. "But, hey, I didn't mean to hold you up, big brother. I'm sure you must be rushing off to an appointment. Did you order?"

"He did." Ingrid spun around so she could grab a to-go cup and suck in a breath. She managed to get his coffee into the cup and snap on the lid without making a mess. Turning back to the counter, she handed it to him.

He reached for his wallet.

"Never mind." Ingrid made a shooing motion. "It's on the house."

Rox gave him a puzzled glance. "That's all you're getting? No bear claw? No chocolate éclair?"

"No time." His smile encompassed them both. "Good seeing you two."

"Wait. I am such a dunce." Rox touched his arm. "Want to hang out and have pizza with us? It's funny, but I totally forgot you'd be right down the hall."

"I will if I can. Lately it seems like emergency calls come in at night, especially on the weekend."

"Well, I hope that doesn't happen. It would be fun to spend a little time with you. We could play *Sorry* if you're there. It's more fun with three. Bring your beer, though. I know wine's not your favorite."

"I'll show up if I can." He touched the brim of his hat. "Ladies."

Rox gazed after him as he barreled out the door. "He's so cute. I'm amazed nobody in this town has snatched him up."

Ingrid's choked inhale set off a small coughing fit. "Probably because he's...always working."

"I know, right?" She peered at Ingrid. "Are you okay? You look a little flushed."

"Just swallowed wrong. I'm fine."

"Well, good. I'm really looking forward to tonight."

"Me, too." It was the first out-and-out lie she'd ever told Rox, but it likely wouldn't be the last.

_19_

Wes pulled out his phone and texted Roxanne that he'd pick up the pizza and order a family size. Then he phoned in the order and pointed his truck in the direction of the pizza parlor for the second time in two days.

Eating the same kind of pizza two nights in a row didn't bother him. He had other, more pressing concerns. Every minute he spent with Roxanne in Ingrid's apartment would increase his chances of accidentally blowing this program to smithereens.

As he'd told Ingrid, he wasn't good at keeping secrets. Gage was a whiz at it, but he was the only one in the family who had that talent. Everyone else tended to forget that something was a secret and blurt it out at exactly the wrong time.

An emergency call could still save him from spending several hours monitoring every word out of his mouth. Gee, didn't that sound like fun? But no call had come in yet. Just when he desperately needed an excuse to bail, his phone had gone silent.

He wouldn't wish an emergency on anyone, but the calls had been so regular. Three Forks had handled two for him last night while he was with Ingrid. Looked like he'd be with her again tonight. Only it wouldn't be quite the same, would it?

Not that he didn't love Roxanne. He adored her. But her timing sucked. Or maybe not. They'd had such a close connection all these years that on some level she could be sensing that his life had changed dramatically in the past week and a half.

Kind of like his sudden urge to visit her in Eagles Nest in March had been prompted by a vague uneasiness and a sudden need to see her. Lo and behold, she'd just become involved with Michael.

She didn't suspect his recent connection with Ingrid, though. If she did, she wouldn't have been so breezy and casual this morning in the bakery. If she'd thought anything was going on, she would have taken him aside right then and there to get the scoop. She wouldn't have been coy about it.

After he picked up the pizza, he stopped by his apartment to drop off his hat and snag the six-pack. It was the same one Ingrid had brought down Thursday night, and it was only minus the one beer he'd opened then.

She'd bought him beer sometime between their encounter on Sunday and Thursday night. At the time, he'd been too tired to have it register, but why had she done that? Had she planned to entertain him in her apartment at some point?

Evidently he hadn't been the only one who'd been hoping they'd escalate the relationship.

As he started down the hall, laughter spilled out of Ingrid's open door. That brightened his mood. He was glad his sister and Ingrid were such good friends even if it complicated the situation now.

He didn't want to take a chance on messing that up. Roxanne had bravely moved to Eagles Nest without knowing a soul. Ingrid had welcomed her and offered friendship. Abigail had, too, but Ingrid had been the key player in Roxanne's early days here.

Although he didn't think Roxanne would be upset about this relationship, he wasn't privy to everything that had transpired between the two women. He'd have to take his cues from Ingrid.

As he approached her open door carrying pizza that smelled exactly like the one from last night, he struggled to block the automatic association. More specifically, the association with making love to her moments after he'd come through the door with said pizza.

At least this one was ginormous, so the look and heft was different. He trusted that Ingrid had taken the box from the previous one to the dumpster. They'd had wine left over but that wouldn't have been a giveaway since she might have bought it for herself.

"I vote for *When Harry Met Sally*." Roxanne's voice drifted out the open door.

"Are you sure you don't want *Toy Story*? We haven't watched it in ages."

He should have guessed it would be one of those two choices on the docket tonight. They were his sister's favorite films.

"But I'm in a Billy Crystal, Meg Ryan mood." Roxanne was sticking to her guns.

Was Ingrid avoiding the romantic movie on purpose? Time to announce his presence. "What about *Alien*?" He walked through the open door. "How about watching that, instead?" He was greeted by a chorus of boos and hisses. He shrugged. "Just a thought."

His sister and Ingrid lounged on the sofa, barefoot and dressed in shorts and tank tops. They'd each pulled their hair back with a scrunchie. Roxanne looked relaxed. On the surface, so did Ingrid, but she avoided glancing straight at him. That was a tell.

"You don't even like *Alien*," Roxanne said. "Oh, yum. That pizza smells delish. Thanks for bringing it. Let's set it on the coffee table. We're eating in front of the TV."

Ingrid picked up the stack of plates and napkins from the coffee table and set them on her lap. "You can stick your beer in the fridge." Her gaze met his but didn't linger.

"Okay." He put down the pizza, carried his beer into the kitchen and took out a bottle before stashing the rest in a vacant spot in her fridge. Might be the same spot she'd had it in originally. The six-pack had come home.

"Oh, Wes," Roxanne called from the living room. "I was telling Ingrid about the big shindig next weekend at the GG. Have you heard about it?"

"Nope." He opened his beer and dropped the cap in the recycling bin before rejoining the women. "Fill me in."

"Next Saturday night the GG is hosting a fundraiser for Raptors Rise. They'll unveil Dad's finished scratchboard project and donate half the night's proceeds to the organization."

"Sounds great. I'll make sure I'm there."

"But what if you get called out?"

"I can arrange to have it covered."

"How?"

"I'll put an out of office message on my phone and direct them to Three Forks."

"What a great idea. Have you done that before?"

"Yes."

"Well, good, then. I'd hate for you to miss this. The Whine and Cheese Club will be serving that night."

"Oh, really?" That surprised him. "Do they have any experience at that?"

"Kendra says they're all rank amateurs. And they'll be wearing bird costumes."

"Of course they will." He hadn't been around for any of their antics other than dancing in the back of Faith's truck on the Fourth. He'd been told that was mild compared to their usual shenanigans. "Can't wait to see how that turns out." He glanced at Ingrid. "You're going, right?"

"Wouldn't miss it."

"You can walk down with me, if you want." He said it as if he didn't care one way or the other.

"Okay, why not?" An appropriately casual response.

"I'm glad I remembered to tell you." Roxanne turned back to the TV. "Come sit down so we can start the movie."

He evaluated the available space. "I'll take the floor." He walked around to the far side of the sofa.

"No, no, come sit with us." Roxanne shifted to one end to make room in the middle. "You can reach the pizza better that way. We can fit, right, Ingrid?"

"Right." She plastered herself against the arm of the sofa on the other end.

He hesitated. Being that close to her was problematic.

"Sit down, Wesley." Roxanne rolled her eyes. "We won't bite."

He settled into the space they'd left him but didn't allow his knee to touch Ingrid's. If he'd been totally relaxed, he wouldn't have worried about it.

"Here's a plate." Ingrid handed him one with a quick glance and a tiny smile. "Get some pizza before we start the movie."

"Yes, ma'am." He returned her smile. Maybe having this secret wasn't all bad. It bonded them.

"Wait, I need more wine." Roxanne picked up a bottle that was almost empty and poured it into her glass. "That kills that one." She reached down beside her and came up with an identical bottle. "Want to top yours off, Ingrid?"

"Sure, thanks."

"Let me do it." He took the bottle from Roxanne, opened it, and poured some in each of the glasses they held out until they told him to stop. He recapped the wine and handed Roxanne the bottle.

She surveyed the arrangement. "Everybody ready? Got pizza? Got your beverage of choice?"

"I'm all set," Ingrid said.

"Roll it, sis." He settled back as much as he dared. His right shoulder was almost touching Ingrid's. Their hips were only a couple of inches apart. If he relaxed his knees, his right one would meet her left one.

They were positioned the same way they had been for the three-legged race, but opposite. She was left-handed and holding her wine glass in that hand. She must have held it that way the night before. And on Sunday, she must have eaten with her left hand. He'd been too focused on the sensual overtones of the meals to catch that.

He looked at her. "I'll try not to bump your arm."

"No worries." She gave him a cute little smile.

"Shh," Roxanne said. "It's starting."

He dipped his head in acknowledgment and lifted his beer bottle in her direction. She touched her wine glass to the side of the bottle. When he checked to see if Roxanne had noticed, she was engrossed in the movie. Didn't matter how many times she'd seen it, she hung on every word of the opening, a montage of long-married couples describing how they'd met and fallen in love.

He liked the opening, too, and watching it with his sister and Ingrid while he drank beer and ate pizza was cozy. At some point his knee settled against Ingrid's and their shoulders nudged up against each other's.

Had they been alone, he would have gathered her closer, but nestling against her, even a little bit, made a nice connection. He could be happy with that until later. She didn't have to get up at three tomorrow morning. That created some interesting possibilities.

He finished his beer and could have used another one, but disturbing the dynamic wasn't worth it. And they'd come to the diner scene. He hadn't forgotten a single thing about what had become the most famous part of the movie.

He and Roxanne had watched the scene together many times. She'd educated him about the practice of women faking orgasms, which had made no sense to him at first. But through personal experience, he'd learned. Incredible though it might be, some women, maybe a lot of women, did it.

Thanks to his sister and Meg Ryan, he could tell the difference. Meg was funny as hell demonstrating the appropriate cries and moans while sitting across from Billy Crystal in a crowded diner. Wes usually got a kick out of it.

Not this time. The noises Meg Ryan made were fake, but they were close enough to the real thing that his cock stirred. Not surprising considering what he and Ingrid had been doing the night before. She shifted her weight. Not much, but enough to signal that she might also be reacting.

Roxanne laughed. "I just love this scene."

"Me, too." Ingrid sounded on the verge of giggles. She set her empty wine glass on the table. "What a classic."

"Yep." A one-word response was the most he could offer under difficult circumstances. He gripped his empty beer bottle and willed his inconvenient erection away.

Then Ingrid nudged his knee with hers.

He glanced at her. Those amazing eyes looked back at him with amusement and understanding. She focused on the screen again, but she slipped her hand into the space between their thighs.

Accepting that subtle invitation, he shifted enough to slide his hand in the gap and lace his fingers through hers. They held hands until the credits rolled. It was the best movie date he'd ever had.

20

After the movie was over, Ingrid pulled out dessert, individual strawberry tarts with whipped cream topping. Wes and Roxanne raved about the tarts and she promised they'd become a staple in the bakery. She'd experimented with them this afternoon after closing.

While enjoying the tarts and coffee, they played a cutthroat game of *Sorry* at the kitchen table. When each of them had won a game, Wes claimed exhaustion. She didn't believe it for a minute.

Roxanne did, though, and said she'd walk him home. He gave Ingrid a quick hug, the kind exchanged by good friends, and walked down the hall with his arm draped casually over his sister's shoulder as they talked in low tones. So far, so good.

But if the evening had gone without a hitch, Ingrid gave most of the credit to Rox's trust in her good friend. She hadn't seen anything amiss because she hadn't been looking for it. Would she understand if Ingrid confessed? Or would she feel betrayed?

Ingrid didn't relish finding out the answer. She ducked back into her apartment to wait. The minute Wes could come to her, he would. But Roxanne might have some things on her mind, subjects she'd rather discuss privately with him.

Or maybe she *had* noticed something tonight and wanted to ask him if anything was going on. Wes wouldn't lie to her and Ingrid wouldn't want him to.

Avoiding detection was one thing. Lying in response to a direct question about their relationship was wrong. She wouldn't do it, either.

Anxiety churned in her stomach. She wouldn't have had to worry about any of this if she'd been up front with everyone from the beginning. Instead, she'd tried to hide her relationship with Wes to prevent complications while she figured things out. Well, she hadn't figured out anything, and this situation was getting more complicated by the minute.

She paced the apartment until a soft rap made her spin toward the open door. "Does she think something's going on?"

"No." Wes walked toward her. "She wanted to discuss Gage. She's been thinking of contacting him to see what's going on with him, but she's decided to hold off for now."

"Oh. All right, then." She sighed. "That's good, I guess, but..."

"What?" He paused, his expression uncertain.

"I'm feeling super guilty about carrying on an affair behind her back."

"Do you want me to call and tell her?" He pulled out his phone. "I doubt she's made it home yet. She could—"

"No!" Her heart rate shot into the stratosphere. "Don't call her. I'm may be feeling guilty, but I'm not ready for that conversation, either."

"What do you want to do?"

"Let's go up on the roof."

"On the *roof*?"

"Yeah, don't you...wait, I forgot. I'll bet Rox didn't mention it because it's never been her thing. Or Abigail's either. And it was too cold when you were here in March, anyway."

"Now I'm curious. What's so great about the roof?"

"It's an awesome place to go when I need to think. All those stars give me perspective."

"How do we get there?"

"Let me grab my shoes and I'll show you." She hurried back to her bedroom, shoved her feet into some canvas deck shoes and came back out.

"Just follow me." She led the way into the hall and over to a narrow door at the end of it. "I discovered this one day by accident." Opening the door, she started up a ladder mounted to the wall of a space a little smaller than her shower stall.

"Good thing I have my phone."

"Why?"

"If I get wedged in here I can call the fire department to drag my ass back out."

"You'll be fine. Hug the ladder on our way up."

"I'd rather hug you."

"Trust me, it's worth the effort." Reaching up, she unfastened the trap door and pushed it open as she climbed the next couple of rungs.

She held onto the latch until she was nearly through. Then she let it down slowly onto the roof's surface so it wouldn't damage the door or the roof. She'd never told the landlady about her trips up here since there was a good chance she'd be asked to stop doing it. Clearly there was a liability issue, but she was always careful.

"Whoever designed this was a lot smaller than I am. I feel like toothpaste being squeezed out of the tube." Wes climbed the rest of the way. "Now we close it, right?"

"I always do." Once he was out she lowered the door into place. "Don't want some poor bat to accidentally fly in." She straightened. "Now look up."

He tilted his head back. "Oh, wow."

"Doesn't it remind you of sugar sprinkled on a chocolate cake?"

He chuckled. "Now it does. I was going with rock salt on wet pavement, but I like your description better." He continued to look upward as he drew in a deep breath. "I used to notice the stars a lot more. Out at the Lazy S they were amazing. But lately I've been so focused on work that I...this is great. Thanks for bringing me up here."

She tugged on his arm. "I have a favorite spot. We can sit and get comfy." She sat on the white-coated tarpaper surface, leaned against a parapet that was about two feet high, and patted the place next to her.

He lowered himself down beside her. "I see we also have a mountain view from here. Nice."

"They're not very distinct at night unless there's a full moon. But they're gorgeous at sunset." She turned to him. "Like it?"

"How could I not? I'm with you." He gazed at her. "But I don't know if I should put my arm around you or not. Are we okay?"

"*We* are. It's just...I'm not sure what to do. But I'd love you to put your arm around me."

"That's a relief." He slipped his arm over her shoulders and scooted closer. "I know we have things to talk out, but I'd much rather do it while I'm holding you."

"Me, too."

"You know, until tonight I didn't really understand what you meant about our situation being complicated. But adding Roxanne to the equation really brought it home. It was sobering."

The guilt returned as she stared up at the stars. "This is my fault. I started this the night I brought you dinner and...stayed. If I hadn't suggested—"

"Hey, don't go taking the blame for this mess. You escalated things that night, but you didn't start anything. I'm the one who pulled you up on my horse, the one who invited myself to be your partner in the three-legged race."

She looked over at him. "But you were just goofing around."

"At first, yeah. But then...I became a lot more focused. I needed to know what your poster was about because I wanted to find out if I had a chance with you."

"I probably shouldn't have given you one. It was too soon."

"Why did you?"

"Because I'm an idiot."

Heat flared in his eyes. "You're not an idiot. You followed your instincts. I'm grateful you took me to bed that night. It was magic. I needed you. Don't spoil it, okay?"

"Okay." She reached up and caressed his cheek. "But having Rox over tonight was tough."

"Does it have to be?" He held her gaze. "Don't you think she'd be happy that we're together?"

"I think she'd be worried about what we're risking—my relationship with her, the great living arrangement above the bakery, co-existing in this small town—it's a lot to put on the line. She'd be worried about that."

"*She'd* be worried about all that?"

"Of course! I don't want to put her through the angst. It's better if she doesn't know what's going on."

"I see." An emotion flashed in his eyes and was gone as quickly as it came, almost as if he'd doused it on purpose. "But it bothers you that we're keeping it a secret from her, doesn't it?"

"Big time. That's why I don't know what to do."

"Want my vote? Let's tell everyone, starting with Roxanne."

Her chest tightened. "I don't think that's a good idea. Not yet."

He studied her. "It won't be as hard as you think."

"It may be even harder! So much could go wrong. We need to wait."

He gazed at her for a long time. Then he reached up and tucked a strand of loose hair behind her ear, his touch sending sparks down her neck. "All right."

She let out a long sigh. He'd agreed. For now, things could continue as they were.

He captured her hand and nibbled on the tips of her fingers. "As I said before, I'll just take my cues from you."

"Then here's one." She scooted around so she had a better angle. Then she cradled the back of his head and leaned in so she could give him a gentle, yet sensual kiss.

"Mm."

She drew back. "Was that clear?"

"Not really." His mouth quirked in a lazy smile. "Better try it again."

"Be glad to." She climbed on his lap and grasped his head with both hands. Lowering her mouth to his, she took it slow at first.

When he cupped her backside, she picked up steam. Straddling his thighs, she rose to her knees and tilted his head back while she kissed him with all the reckless abandon he inspired in her.

His fingers tightened as a low groan rose from his throat. The desperation in that sound arrowed straight to her core. She lifted her mouth a fraction from his and gasped for breath. "I ache for you."

"Good." His voice was rough with passion. "That's a problem I can fix."

"Here?"

His chuckle rasped in the silence. "At seventeen I would have." Lifting her away, he got to his feet and helped her up. "But we can do better than that."

Their descent down the ladder was pure slapstick because they were in a hurry. He insisted she go first because it was the gentlemanly thing to do. She stood outside in the hall while he latched the trap door and started down, his laughter choked and breathless. "My package is *so* unhappy."

"Your choice. We could've—"

"We could've, but I want more options."

Her heart hammered in anticipation. "Do you, now?"

"Yes, ma'am." He came through the door and turned to close it behind him. Then he faced her. "For one thing, I get to do this." Scooping her into his arms, he walked into her apartment and straight back to her bedroom.

"And it thrills me every time."

"Yeah?" He laid her on the bed and followed her down, nuzzling her throat, sliding his hand under her tank top. "Even that first time in the park?"

"Uh-huh." His touch ignited little fires as he unfastened the front catch of her bra and stroked her breasts.

"Then I'm glad we didn't finish that race the right way." Working her top up, he pulled it over her head and tossed it aside. Then he pushed her bra away and his hot gaze traveled over all that he'd revealed.

Her nipples tightened and her skin grew warm.

"I love when that happens." He cupped a breast in each hand. "When you turn that pretty shade of pink and your nipples pucker. It's like an invitation."

Her breathing quickened. "It is an invitation."

"Then I accept." Leaning down, he drew one tight bud into his mouth.

She closed her eyes. So good. Sliding her fingers into his silky hair, she held him to her breast and gasped as the sweet suction traveled straight to her aching core. Moisture gathered between her thighs and she moaned.

Approval rumbled in his throat as he sucked harder and she began to pant. He unbuttoned her shorts, drew the zipper down and slid his hand inside her panties. With the first thrust of his fingers, she arched off the bed with a cry and spun into the wild vortex of a climax.

He continued to caress her until she sank slowly back to the mattress, her body trembling.

Then at last he lifted his head and looked down at her. The heat in his eyes had turned them almost black. "You drive me crazy." His voice was thick with emotion. "I can't even tell you how much—"

"You don't have to." She gulped for air. "I can see it."

"I want you to feel it, too." Leaving the bed, he stripped down and tore open a condom he pulled from the pocket of his jeans.

She took off her shorts and panties with quivering hands. No one had ever wanted her this much.

He came back to bed and moved between her thighs. "Ingrid, I'm shaking."

"Me, too."

Bracing his forearms on either side of her, he met her gaze. "I don't shake when I make love. Except with you."

She quivered for an entirely different reason. He was saying far more than his words conveyed. And it scared the hell out of her. She wrapped her arms around him, pulling him closer.

His chest heaved. "What we have means a lot to me."

Her throat thickened and she swallowed to clear it. "I know. Me, too."

"I believe you." He entered her slowly as tremors shook him. But when he was locked in tight, the tremors stopped. Leaning down, he brushed a kiss over her lips. "That's why I'm here."

I believe you. As he began to love her, gently and thoroughly, she surrendered to another glorious climax. He gave without holding back. But could she ever do the same?

21

Wes's phone chimed as he lay on his back, heart pounding and breath unsteady from the power of sharing an orgasm with Ingrid. Rolling to his side, he reached toward the nightstand and almost knocked the phone to the floor. He managed to answer before it went to voicemail.

A mare he'd been monitoring ever since he'd started taking clients a month ago was in labor. He'd promised to be there. After assuring the worried owners that he'd arrive in twenty minutes, he disconnected and turned back to Ingrid. "I have to go."

"I heard." She smiled. "The timing could have been worse."

"A lot worse." He gave her a quick kiss and climbed out of bed so he could dispose of the condom and pull on his briefs and jeans. "But wouldn't you know, just when you're able to sleep in..."

"Oh, don't worry. I'll still sleep in."

"Yes, but I wanted to sleep in with you, smarty pants." He buttoned his jeans and tugged up the zipper.

"Maybe next Saturday night, after the thing at the Guzzling Grizzly."

"It's a deal." He picked up his shirt and his boots. "I was going to have my out of office message turned on anyway, so I'll just extend the time until noon on Sunday."

"Sounds decadent."

"Plan on it. We'll eat chocolate eclairs in bed. But I'll see you long before then. It's about time for this deluge of appointments to taper off. I'll be back here before you have time to miss me."

"Hope so."

"I'll make it a priority."

* * *

He'd had to eat his words. By three o'clock on Thursday afternoon, when he'd only interacted with Ingrid briefly while getting coffee and pastries at Pie in the Sky each morning, his Saturday night boast had come back to haunt him.

He'd exchanged a few texts with her, but tentative plans to get together had been blown apart by his crazy schedule. The appointments had come thick and fast. On top of that, he'd responded to medical emergencies every single night. Was it a universal truth that emergencies only cropped up after hours?

Being short on sleep and short on Ingrid's kisses was a bad combo. He'd solve one of those problems today. He left a client's place at three-thirty and the bakery closed at four. Although she didn't normally work that last hour, she often came down to help Abigail close.

Sure, he could text instead of going in person, but he needed to see her. He was sick of communicating via text. And he could use a cup of coffee.

He planned to go in, place an order and casually find out if she had any obligations for the rest of the day. If she didn't, he'd claim an hour of her time. Or more if she'd let him. He'd turn on the out of office message on his phone. He was a desperate man.

He must have looked desperate, too, because when he walked up to the pastry counter and asked Abigail for a couple of brownies, she gave him a worried look. "Are you okay?"

"Oh, yeah. Nothing some sugar and caffeine can't cure." He'd deliberately chosen to order brownies first, so he wouldn't appear too eager about being served coffee by Ingrid. He was the only customer. If someone else came in to draw Abigail's attention, that would help.

"Want one of Ingrid's Firecrackers? Those triple espressos could take rust off a tailpipe. "

"Just plain coffee should do it."

"You got it. For here or to go?"

"Here." He sighed and tilted back his hat. "No more appointments today. Unless something unexpected comes up."

"Then take a load off and relax, cowboy." She raised her voice. "Ingrid, your neighbor wants a regular coffee. He'll have it here."

"I'm on it. Hey, Wes. How's it going?"

"Good." *Have you missed me as much as I've missed you? Do you feel as if somebody has lopped off a whole chunk of your life? Because that's the way I feel.*

"Here are your brownies." Abigail slid a china plate across the top of the bakery case and handed him a napkin.

"Thanks." After paying, he sauntered over to the coffee counter as if his heart hadn't turned into a Mexican jumping bean. "Busy day?"

"Fairly busy. Not like you, though." She set the brimming mug of coffee in front of him and glanced up.

His breath caught. So beautiful. His chest tightened with longing.

She gave him a soft smile. "Better drink your coffee before it gets cold."

"Right." And snap out of his daze. If Abigail had noticed him staring at Ingrid like that, she'd make the correct assumption.

So much for finding a creative way to ask if she was free after the bakery closed. Texting would be safer than prolonging the conversation and struggling to be clever. He picked up his mug. "Thanks."

"You bet." With another quick smile, she turned away.

He sighed. She couldn't be caught staring at him, either. He hated this. Disguising their feelings for each other sucked. He was ready for it to end.

As he headed for a table with his coffee and brownies, a tall cowboy walked in. Wes blinked. Couldn't be.

But it was. That cocky grin belonged to none other than his vagabond brother Gage.

The grin turned to laughter. "You should see your face, little brother! Wish I'd had my phone ready. That would've made a hilarious picture."

Wes slopped his coffee as he put it back on the counter along with the plate of brownies. "I can't believe this." He strode over and gave his brother a tight hug. "Have you been out to Dad's? Does he know you're in town? Are you—"

"Whoa, whoa. Don't hurt yourself. Haven't been to Dad's, yet. I took a chance and stopped here, first. Hoped you might be around and sure, enough. You must be in hog heaven living over a bakery."

A heaven that had recently turned into a frustrating hell. "It suits me fine. Let me introduce you to these two ladies, the best bakers I've ever known." When he glanced back, they were watching the drama with obvious interest. "Abigail and Ingrid—" He gestured to each one in turn. "Meet my long-lost brother Gage."

"Glad to make your acquaintance, Miss Abigail and Miss Ingrid." Gage tipped his hat.

"It's good to finally meet you, too, Gage." Abigail smiled at him. "I've heard rumors about a third Sawyer brother but I was beginning to think you were an urban myth."

"No, ma'am. I may be legendary, but I do, in fact, exist. And although my sweet tooth isn't nearly as developed as Wesley's, I wouldn't mind joining him for some coffee and brownies." He glanced around. "Although from the look of things you might be getting ready to close."

"We close at four, but we won't kick you out," Abigail said. "It's not every day another Sawyer turns up."

"Well, I'm the last of the litter, so if another joker rides into town claiming to be a Sawyer, he's an imposter."

Abigail laughed. "I'll keep that in mind. How many brownies would you like?"

"A dozen, if you have that many. And a dozen chocolate chip cookies, too, so I have some goodies to take out to my dad's." He looked over at Wes. "I was hoping I could talk you into going out there with me after we gird our loins with coffee and brownies."

"I can do that."

"What kind of coffee do you want, Gage?" Ingrid swept a hand toward the menu on the wall. "We have plenty of options."

"You certainly do." He rubbed his chin. "I'll have one of those Firecrackers, please, ma'am."

Wes chuckled. "Same old Gage."

"No point in drinking coffee unless it's gonna put hair on your chest."

"Then you made the right choice." Ingrid glanced at Wes. "I'll get you a fresh cup."

"You know what? I'll take a Firecracker, too, if you don't mind."

Her eyes widened. "Are you sure?"

"I'm sure." Might as well get his kicks where he could. The way this afternoon was shaping up, he wouldn't be enjoying a secret rendezvous with her anytime soon.

"Alrighty, then. Please have a seat. I'll bring them to you."

"Okay." Wes picked up his plate of brownies. "Thanks, Ingrid."

"You're welcome." She flashed him a warm smile.

"See that?" Gage punched him lightly on the shoulder as they walked over to a table.

"See what?" If Gage had sensed the vibe between him and Ingrid...

"I'm in town ten minutes and I'm already a bad influence on you. Now you're ordering triple-shot lattes."

"Yeah, you're a terrible influence." Whew. Disaster averted. "I've missed you."

"Missed you, too, big guy." He took the small bistro chair across from Wes. It didn't fit Gage any better than it did him. "I thought it wouldn't bother me, Dad selling the Lazy S. I mean, I haven't lived there for years and lately I haven't been home much. But still..."

"Not surprising you'd feel weird about it. It's where we grew up."

Gage's jaw dropped in pretend shock. "You noticed that, *too*? But then you've always been smart. Makes sense you'd become a doctor. Which reminds me, I have this pain in my gluteus maximus and I—"

"I'm sure you do." He laughed because Gage was funny, but his pattern was achingly familiar. Whenever he was worried that he'd revealed more than he'd intended, he started cracking jokes. Wes pushed his plate to the middle of the table. "Take one of these and call me in the morning."

"Don't mind if I do. Thanks." He picked up a brownie and bit into it.

"How long are you here for?"

He chewed and swallowed. "That's yet to be determined."

"You don't have a job?"

"Not at the moment." He took another bite of the brownie.

"Did you get fired?"

He rolled his eyes and finished chewing. "No, I did not. I've only been fired that one time. It so happens I quit my current job."

"In the middle of the busy season?" Wes was used to Gage's erratic behavior but this wasn't smart. A wrangler had to make money when he or she was in demand, which would be now.

"I—" He glanced up as Ingrid came over with their coffee drinks. "Ah, thank you, ma'am. I'm looking forward to this."

She set one in front of each of them. "I'd advise taking it slow."

"And I second that." Abigail showed up with two more brownies on a plate for Gage and a bakery box. "There's a reason we posted a warning for that one."

Gage smiled. "That's why I got it." He took a hefty swallow.

Wes could do no less. He didn't choke, but the effort not to made his eyes water. Across the table, Gage was in the same fix. And red in the face. Wes figured he was, too.

Ingrid and Abigail ducked their heads and there was much throat-clearing going on between the two of them. Abigail excused herself and left but Ingrid remained.

She had every right to stay and gloat. She'd warned them. And maybe, just maybe, she was using this as an excuse to be near him.

He dragged in a breath. "Great stuff."

"You said it, bro." Gage coughed once. "Excellent brew, Ingrid."

"Glad you like it." Her eyes gleamed with mischief as she looked over at Wes. "I could start another one for each of you if you'd like."

"Thanks," Wes said, "but we'll be shoving off soon." Right after they finished guzzling their jet fuel. "Have you tried this?"

"Of course. I invented it."

"Respect." Gage hoisted his mug in her direction. "You have talent and guts, ma'am."

"Thank you. I'll leave you to enjoy your coffee." She returned to her spot behind the counter.

"So that's how it is."

Wes's gaze snapped to his brother's. "I don't—"

He leaned closer and lowered his voice. "I highly approve, not that you need my approval. She's great. And a baker. Perfect for you."

Denying it was pointless. Gage had come into the situation with no preconceived ideas. That allowed him to see what others couldn't. "Nobody's supposed to know."

Gage's eyebrows lifted.

"She's Roxanne's best friend."

"That should be a plus."

"It's not."

"Okay. We'll talk later."

"But don't say anything to the others."

"I won't." He picked up his coffee and took a more conservative swallow. Even then, he gave a little cough afterward. "Epic brew."

"Yep."

"Listen, I need your advice. Speaking of keeping things quiet, I'm not planning to tell anyone else."

"Okay."

"I've saved a little money and I've decided to take a break and figure some things out. I'm— don't laugh—thinking about settling down."

"I'm not laughing. That sounds great."

"There's this woman I spent some time with about a year and a half ago when I was working at a ranch outside of Great Falls. We got along well, extremely well, but you know me. I felt the walls closing in and took off."

"Uh-huh."

"I think that was a mistake. But it's been a year and a half. Should I forget her or go see her?"

"Neither. Call her."

He shook his head. "It's too easy to say no on the phone. If she doesn't want to have anything to do with me, I want her to say it to my face, look me in the eye." He took a breath. "Or I could just forget the whole thing."

"I don't think you will."

"You're right." He heaved a sigh. "I'll go see her. Then at least I won't be in limbo."

"Limbo's not good." And he couldn't live that way much longer, either.

Gage's sudden arrival had focused a spotlight on what he wanted. Or maybe it was the Firecracker's caffeine running through his system, turning him into a human lightbulb.

In any case, he'd gained a new perspective. He just had to figure out what to do about it.

After he and Gage finished their lattes and said goodbye to Ingrid and Abigail, he led the way out to their dad's place. He'd tried to talk Gage into texting to find out if their dad was even home. He could be over at Kendra's, or out at Roxanne and Michael's building site checking on the progress. He could even be working on his latest art project, although probably not. Mornings were his creative time.

But Gage was all about just showing up. He liked to surprise people, which was interesting because when the family had given him a surprise party for his sixteenth birthday, he'd freaked out.

Pete wouldn't be home yet, and Roxanne hardly ever stopped by, busy as she was with her graphic design projects and the new house going up. Gage might have no one to greet him besides Fudge, Clifford and Banjo. Not that it was likely to bother Gage one bit. After he'd said hello to the horses, he'd probably kick back in one of the rockers on the porch and invite Wes to join him while they waited. At least Wes had a key to the house.

Then he spotted his dad's truck parked in its usual place by the barn. Good. His dad had been worrying about Gage and seeing him this afternoon would be a big deal. Yeah, the plan to spend time with Ingrid had been torpedoed, but it was a small sacrifice in the grand scheme. The payoff for his dad would be huge.

He pulled in and shut off the motor. Gage parked beside him just as his dad walked out of the barn, no doubt to ID his visitors. He lifted a hand in greeting as Wes climbed down from the cab.

Then he paused, shoved back his hat and stared in the direction of the other truck. "What the hell? Gage?"

"Hey, Dad." He swung down and came around the back of his truck.

Wes decided to stay put and let the reunion play out. It was a great show. Both men wore big grins as they quickly closed the distance, although his dad's smile looked a little wobbly.

As they embraced, Wes choked up some, too. The Sawyer clan had been a close family until all the kids except Pete had left the Lazy S to chase their dreams. Gage had made the biggest break, rarely visiting since he'd taken off at the age of eighteen.

Stepping back and clearing his throat, his dad surveyed Gage with a fond expression. "You seem to be holding up okay."

"Thanks." Gage smiled. "I manage."

"To what do we owe the honor of your presence?"

"I was in the neighborhood."

"Likely story. Did you tell Wes that you were—"

"No, sir, he had no prior knowledge. I showed up at the bakery about an hour ago and ambushed him."

"Well, whatever your reasons, I'm glad to see you, son. Everybody else will be, too. Let's go grab some cold ones and I'll start making calls." He ushered them into the house and pulled beer out of the fridge before he picked up his phone.

In no time the house turned into party central. Kendra came over first, followed by Roxanne and Michael not long afterward. Pete showed up last and gave Gage some good-natured hell for dropping in unannounced.

Everybody pitched in to get a meal going as conversation and laughter flowed. All of Wes's favorite peeps were finally gathered under one roof. All except one.

She could have been here, too, since her work was over for the day. She would have fit in so well with this crowd. Her name even came up when Gage regaled the group with a description of her Firecracker latte. Nobody besides Gage and Wes had tried it.

Pete and Michael vowed to order one soon, as if downing a Firecracker had become a test of manly courage. Ingrid would get a kick out of that. She was missing out by not being here, damn it.

He'd understood her need for discretion in the beginning but tonight it weighed him down like an anchor around his neck. Yes, she was gun-shy after what had happened with her last relationship, but he wasn't her ex. Their situation was completely different. Keeping their affair secret from his family, people he loved and trusted, didn't sit well.

He'd talk to her about it tomorrow, get things out in the open. Gage had picked up on the emotional currents running between him and Ingrid without knowing anything about the situation. That would only be possible if those emotions ran deep. Ingrid might not be ready to admit it, but he was. Gage's confirmation had convinced him it was time to shake things up.

22

The text from Wes dropped into Ingrid's phone at three-thirty in the morning as she was getting ready for work.

I need to see you today. Can you give me a little time during your morning break? So we can talk?

And what could he want to talk about? The answer was obvious. He was frustrated with the status quo. He'd radiated it yesterday when he'd come in, probably to arrange a chance to see each other. Then Gage had arrived.

Well, Wes wasn't the only one who was frustrated. She hadn't been sleeping well, and watching him walk out of the bakery with his brother had put her in a funk for the rest of the evening. They had a plan for Saturday night and Sunday morning, but she didn't want to wait that long, either.

Can you meet me in my apartment at ten-thirty this morning?

His answer was immediate.

I'll be there.

Good. They had a plan. But instead of helping her anxiety, tension wrapped a tight band around her skull, pressing against her temples and giving her a mild headache.

If only they'd connected this week. Then neither of them would be in this fix. But he was building a clientele, and sacrifices had to be made. Keeping their relationship secret—her rule—added another layer of stress.

By the time ten-thirty rolled around and she walked out of the bakery, she was a bundle of nerves. His dusty truck was in its parking space so he was already up there waiting. Joy had been the driving force behind their interactions...until now.

She clutched her phone in one hand as she climbed the stairs. The timer was set so she wouldn't be late getting back to work. She stepped into the hall.

He stood just outside her door. Then she was in his arms, his hungry mouth capturing hers.

Her anxiety melted in an avalanche of warmth, caring and passion. So much passion. He groaned and pulled her tight, fitting his hips to hers, letting her know how much he wanted her.

He lifted his mouth a fraction from hers. "I've missed you like the devil."

"I've missed you, too. And Saturday night we—"

"I can't live this way."

She went very still. "What?"

He closed his eyes and groaned. "Sorry. That wasn't how I planned to open the discussion."

"But it's open, now." Her blood had been racing with excitement. Now it slowed, chilled by his pronouncement. "Do you want to have it here or—"

"In your apartment." Releasing her, he took her hand and squeezed it. "We'll work this out. I know we can."

She hoped he was right. They walked into her living room and took a seat on the sofa, still holding hands, their bodies angled toward each other, their opposite knees touching. "Before we start, do you notice anything missing in this room?"

"Missing?" He frowned. "Like what?"

"The poster."

He glanced across the room at the blank wall. "I'll be damned. You'd think I'd have seen that first thing."

She smiled. "You'd think."

"When did you take it down?"

"Sunday. I wasn't in the mood for that message anymore."

"That's encouraging." He gazed at her. "Does that mean you're ready to talk with Roxanne?"

The band tightened around her skull. "No, it doesn't. The event at the GG tomorrow night is a big deal and I'm not going to risk upsetting her before a fundraiser Michael's orchestrating, a night that's also special for your dad. I—"

"How do you think she'll feel when she finds out after the fact?"

"What do you mean?"

"I spent last night with my family, including Michael and Kendra. When Gage showed up, everyone gathered. It was a special time and I wanted you there, too. If we weren't hiding our relationship, you could've been."

"But I'm not part of—"

"Aren't you? You said this was important to you, that *I'm* important to you."

"You are!"

"How can I be when nobody knows about this except us?"

"They will know. In due time."

"How much time?"

"I can't say, all right? This is tricky."

"What if I talk to her?"

She gulped as a wave of panic hit her. "No, please don't. It's my job. I need to be the one to talk with her. Now is not the right time."

"Why not? What if every day you procrastinate you—"

"I'm not procrastinating! I'm being considerate of Rox's feelings."

"Is it really her feelings you're worried about? You're so sure she's going to be upset when she finds out. What if she's thrilled?"

"Thrilled? How could she be? We've been carrying on behind her back. She'll be upset. Probably hurt. Or angry. I don't want to do that to her."

"That doesn't sound like Roxanne, and you know it. But it reminds me of someone else." He pulled his hands away from hers. "You want to know what I think this is really about? That!" He pointed at the empty place on her wall where the poster had hung. "I think you're holding out to see if I turn into a jerk like your ex."

"That's not it at all!" She pressed a hand to her chest. If only her heart would stop making so much noise. "Wes, we're fighting."

"We're *discussing*."

"No, we're not. We're fighting. And if we keep fighting, everything's going to blow apart."

"I disagree. We can work this out. You know me. You know my heart. I won't—"

"Please, Wes, we have to stop."

"Thank you, Lord! That's what I've been saying. We'll tell everyone and be done with the secrecy."

"That's not what I meant."

He gazed at her in silence. Then he swallowed. "What did you mean?"

She forced the words out. "We have to stop this. Us. Now, before anyone knows." Such hateful words.

He recoiled as if she'd slapped him. Pain flashed in his eyes. "You can't be serious."

"It's the only way. If we end this now, we can still be…friends."

"*Friends?*" Drawing in a shaky breath, he reached for her hands. "I want so much more from you than friendship. And I think you do, too. I know you care about me, Ingrid, as much as I care about you. And I know those feelings scare the hell out of you."

"I'm not scare—"

"It's understandable after what happened with your ex. But *I'm* not him. *We're* not you and him. Gage was in the bakery five minutes and figured out we're crazy about each other. This will work out."

Gage knew? Panic set in. "No, it won't."

His grip tightened when she tried to pull back. "Come with me to the event Saturday. Please. Be my date. Trust me. Trust *us.*"

The idea of going public made her sick to her stomach. "You don't know what you're asking."

"I'm asking you to trust me. Trust that I won't let you down. Ever. It'll be okay."

"No." Her voice was a hoarse croak. "We have to end this now!" Because if they didn't, she was going to come apart at the seams.

He stared at her for a long time. She counted breaths. It was the only thing that kept her tethered to her sanity.

Heaving a sigh, he released her hands and stood. "If that's what you really want, I'll go. I never meant to hurt you."

And she'd never meant to hurt him. But she had. The pain in his eyes hit her like a sledgehammer. "I'm sorry, Wes."

"Yeah. Me, too." He walked out the door without looking back.

Clutching her knees, she sucked in air. It was like breathing through a straw. She couldn't get enough. Her vision blurred.

What was that music? Oh. Her phone alarm. She had five minutes. She choked back hysterical laughter.

Anyone who could go down to the bakery and carry on as if nothing had happened deserved an academy award. She wasn't that person.

She was shaking like crazy, so texting took longer than it should have. Eventually she composed a message to Abigail explaining that she had stomach flu. Amazing that her brain was working well enough to come up with that.

It didn't feel like a lie, either. The way her stomach was churning, she might throw up. Stomach flu was the perfect illness to fake. She could hide out and ask everyone to stay away. Nobody wanted to catch stomach flu.

Only thing was, it usually lasted just a couple of days, three at most. That would get her out of the celebration at the GG, and Sunday the bakery was closed. Monday morning, though, Tuesday at the latest, she'd have to be on the job.

And every time she left her apartment, she'd have to face the possibility of running into Wes, whether he still came into the bakery for coffee and a pastry or not. They lived in the same building. She'd have to walk past his apartment on a regular basis, each time taking a chance that she'd see him.

And that was just for starters. The future looked even bleaker. Whenever she spent time with Rox, she'd likely hear about what Wes was doing. If he started dating someone, which would happen eventually, she'd hear about that, too. He might even bring his new girlfriend up to his apartment.

The very thing she'd feared had come to pass, despite all her precautions. Life as she knew it was over. She was now officially in hell.

23

Although Wes had wanted business to slow down this past week, today he was grateful for every call that took him away from the apartment building. And the bakery. What a mess.

He should have seen it coming. But when Ingrid had decided to make love to him that first night, he'd wanted so desperately to believe in...what? Her? The healing power of love?

It was powerful, all right, though not at healing. It had grabbed him by the heart and had a substantial grip on his privates, too. Ingrid, not so much. Bottom line, she didn't trust him not to hurt her.

Worse yet, she wouldn't admit that was the issue. She'd offloaded all her concerns onto Roxanne, claiming that they couldn't go public because it would cause Roxanne distress.

That sucked and he didn't know how to fix it. He couldn't just explain it to her. If she didn't trust him with her heart, why would she trust him to tell her the truth about what was happening?

The only person he could talk to was no expert on the matter, either. But when he found himself at loose ends, he texted Gage.

What are you up to?

Enjoying a brewsky on the porch. Come on over.

Is Dad with you?

Nope. He's over at Kendra's for a little private time.

Pete?

Working late.

I'll see you in ten minutes.

He had some munchies in his apartment but no beer. That was still at Ingrid's and he'd never restocked his fridge. Hadn't felt the need. He wasn't going to risk running into her for a bag of pretzels and some mixed nuts.

As he pulled up in front of his dad's house, he smiled for the first time since leaving Ingrid's apartment. Gage had turned front porch beer consumption into an art form.

He'd pulled one of the rockers over to the railing so he could prop his feet on it. On his left sat a small galvanized tub filled with ice and several longnecks. On the other, a table held his phone, a large bowl of tortilla chips, a smaller one of salsa, and a generous basket of popcorn.

A flock of sparrows took off when Wes pulled in. Gage had never met a bird he didn't like, and tossing chips and popcorn to them was a signature activity. Wes had missed that about him, too. Whatever impulse had motivated him to recalibrate his life, Wes was glad that he'd decided to rejoin the family while he did it.

Swinging down from the truck, he climbed the steps. "It's a damned shame you've never learned how to relax."

"Isn't it, though?" Gage tipped back his hat and looked up at him. "But I figure if I keep practicing, I'll get the hang of it. I would've pulled up a rocker for you, but that would require getting up."

"Please don't trouble yourself." Wes grabbed a rocker and positioned it on the far side of the table. "Can you spare one of those longnecks?"

"Got one here with your name on it."

"Thanks." He took the chilled bottle and glanced at the label. "Just call me Bud for short." Propping his feet on the rail, he twisted off the cap and took a long drag on his beer.

"So, Bud, how's Ingrid?"

He damn near spewed the entire mouthful. Somehow he managed to swallow it without choking to death.

"Wrong question?"

Wes gazed at him and cleared his throat. "What are you, psychic?"

"Yeah, but I didn't need to use my powers this time." He broke off a corner of a chip and threw it over the rail. "The bakery closes at four." He tossed out another piece. "At five you're texting me, looking for company. Doesn't take a crystal ball to figure out there's trouble in paradise."

"You can say that again."

"Sorry, but I don't make a habit of repeating myself." He scattered a handful of popcorn and the little birds went crazy. "Share, guys." He turned to Wes. "So are you gonna tell me about it or would you rather play twenty questions?"

"This stays between us."

"Yeah, yeah, we established that yesterday. Cut to the chase. Or in this case, the train wreck."

Wes filled him in. Like the great listener he was, Gage winced and groaned at all the appropriate places in the story. The lead weight in Wes's gut lightened considerably as he talked.

He finished describing the morning's debacle and took a restorative gulp of beer. "There you have it."

"Have you considered talking to Roxanne?"

"No."

"Why not?"

"For one thing, I promised I wouldn't. For another, it wouldn't fix the problem. If Ingrid doesn't trust me to be a good guy and not hurt her, then nothing I say or Roxanne says will make any difference. End of story."

"I doubt that." Gage broke up another chip and gave it to the birds.

"I don't know. Seems like an impasse to me."

"That's because you're the poor slob who's in love with her. Looking at it from the outside, I see potential for it working out."

"Is there something I should be doing?"

Gage turned to stare at him. "You're asking me? The guy who's never had a romance that lasted more than two weeks?"

"I don't have anybody else I can ask."

"That's a shame. I haven't the foggiest idea whether there's something you should do."

"But you're sitting over there saying you see potential for it working out. What the hell is that supposed to mean?"

"That I believe your awesomeness will win out. You're honest, you're loyal, and you floss. She couldn't find a better guy than you and she strikes me as an intelligent woman."

"Thanks." Wes took a quick sip of beer to cover the rush of emotion that little speech had created. "Appreciate it."

"If you'd just learn to put the TP roll on correctly you'd be damned near perfect."

He grinned. "I'm grateful you're here to point out my failings in that department."

"Yeah, me, too." He glanced over at Wes, his expression serious for a change. "Me, too."

* * *

The next morning, Wes was in a considerably better mood. Pete had come home and joined them on the porch. Then they'd cooked dinner and talked far into the night. Like old times.

Gage was sounding as if he might stick around Eagles Nest. He liked what he'd seen of the town and wanted to be involved in Raptors Rise. Pete evidently loved his job and Wes's growing list of clients meant he could afford to stay.

The move from Spokane to Eagles Nest was looking good for the Sawyer clan. The situation with Ingrid had to work out. It just had to.

As Wes showered, shaved and dressed, he focused on Gage's belief that she'd decide to trust the relationship and talk with Roxanne. What if, after taking a night to think it over, she'd decided to call Roxanne today?

She likely wouldn't tell him until after the fact, but the wheels might already be in motion. What if this day would be a turning point and they'd enjoy a wonderful evening together, after all?

He had twenty minutes before his first appointment, enough time for a brief stop at the bakery. He'd have a chance to gauge her mood while he ordered his usual coffee and pastry. Grabbing his keys and his hat, he went quickly down the stairs, eager to see her.

Except she wasn't there. She was always there this time of the morning. Concern jacked up his pulse rate. *Settle down.* He took a deep breath.

Maybe she was on an early break for some reason. She could be running a quick errand at Pills and Pop. Or checking whether she'd turned off the coffee maker in her apartment.

Abigail was busy making pies, so he ordered his bear claw from Yolanda and walked over to the coffee counter. Maybe if he hung around for a few minutes, Ingrid would show up.

He gave his order to Doug, her assistant barista. "I guess Ingrid's on break, huh?" *Keep it casual, Sawyer.*

"Actually, she's not feeling well."

"Oh?" His pulse rate shot up again. "That's too bad."

"Yeah, being sick is no fun." Doug gave him a polite smile as he handed over the coffee in a to-go cup and turned to the next customer in line.

Wes checked the time. He could afford to sit for a couple of minutes and drink his coffee while he kept an eye on Abigail. Maybe she'd come up to the counter after she'd put the pies in the oven.

He'd just taken a sip of coffee when she walked over to say something to Yolanda. He swallowed quickly and set down the cup before he made a beeline for the counter. "Abigail?"

"Hey, Wes." She appeared frazzled. As well she would be without her trusty assistant baker.

"Is Ingrid okay? Doug said she—"

"Stomach flu, poor woman." Abigail made a face. "She doesn't expect to make it tonight and I know she was really looking forward to it."

"Yeah, she was." Stomach flu? He doubted it.

"She wants everyone to leave her to her misery, so I'm respecting that."

"Sure. Of course. Thanks for the info. If you talk to her, please tell her I hope she gets better soon."

"I will. She should be fine by Monday."

"Yes, ma'am." Again, doubtful. He returned to the table to pick up his coffee and the rest of his bear claw so he could head out to his appointment.

She didn't have stomach flu. She was holed up in her apartment, hiding from the world. Hiding from him.

And hurting. Before he climbed into his truck, he glanced up at the second floor of the building. Her apartment didn't have any windows facing the street, but he looked up there, anyway.

Ingrid, don't do this to yourself. If only he could march up there, take her in his arms and make everything all right. But he didn't have that power.

With a sigh, he got into his truck, checked the rearview mirror and backed out. Until talking with Abigail, he'd been basking in the ray of sunshine Gage had offered. That was gone. The lead weight in his stomach had returned, heavier than ever.

24

It all came down to self-respect. Although Ingrid was scared to death that one wrong move could take things from bad to catastrophic, she couldn't live with herself if she missed the Raptors Rise fundraiser at the Guzzling Grizzly.

The *get well soon* texts had been arriving in a steady stream all day. Someone with stomach flu wouldn't have had the strength to answer them all, so she only responded to Abigail, Roxanne and Kendra.

But she read and reread the ones from the McGavin brothers and the Whine and Cheese ladies. Badger came up with a funny video. Nicole embedded a clip from a song. Michael and Luke went the virtual flower route. Even Pete texted her. Not Wes, of course, or Gage. Wes had likely told him what was going on.

But Quinn's text was the clincher, the one that propelled her out of her funk and into the shower. He sent a sketch of her posing as a blonde Rosie the Riveter with *You can do it!* printed underneath.

He'd probably meant she could lick this flu bug, but she chose to make it her mantra for diving back into the community she loved. She would support her friends tonight.

She had just enough time to get ready, although arriving a little late would be smart. Her newfound bravery didn't extend to meeting Wes coming out of his apartment on his way to the event.

To guarantee that didn't happen, she left her door open a crack and finished putting on her makeup in the living room so she could hear him going down the stairs. Then she'd be free to head out. She'd boosted her confidence with a sparkly red top, rhinestone-spangled jeans and red boots she saved for special occasions.

When Wes's door opened with its distinctive creak, she held her breath and waited. The door closed and the clipped beat of his descent echoed in the stairwell. She let out her breath.

The rhythmic sound stopped and went in reverse. He was coming back up. Maybe he'd forgotten something. She swallowed. *Leave, okay?*

She waited for the creak of hinges that indicated he was fetching whatever he'd forgotten. Instead he came down the hall. Her hands trembled as she twisted her lipstick back into the tube and set it aside.

He stopped outside her door. "Ingrid, I wish you'd come to this thing tonight. I hate that you're missing it because of what's going on with us."

She pressed a hand to her mouth and closed her eyes as his voice flowed around her, so warm and caring.

He heaved a sigh. "I hope to see you there." He walked away, and this time he continued down the stairs and out the street door.

You can't be serious.

The desperation in his statement had been ringing in her ears ever since yesterday morning. Desperation and yearning.

I'm asking you to trust me. Trust that I won't let you down. Ever.

She managed to put her lipstick on even though her hand was trembling. Picking up her purse, she left her apartment.

* * *

Laughter and music filtered out the open door of the GG as she approached. Someone had decided to leave it propped open. She'd chosen to walk down and was glad she had. The lot was packed and the aerobic exercise had been exactly what she'd needed.

Taking a deep breath, she braced herself for whatever she'd encounter and stepped inside.

"Ingrid!"

She turned at the sound of Kendra's voice. But instead of Kendra, she was greeted by a giant golden eagle.

Kendra's blue eyes peeked out of the face mask. "I didn't expect to see you here! How are you?"

"Much better. What a gorgeous costume."

"Isn't it?" She spread her arms and gave a little flap to her wings. "Mandy made one for each of us and they're all different. She tried so hard to finish them before the parade. Didn't happen. Come on, let me find you a place."

"I don't see very many empty chairs. I could sit at the bar if—"

"Not necessary. Quinn saved me a seat next to him, but there's no way I'll be sitting down tonight." She threaded her way through the tables.

Ingrid followed, her chest tightening more with every step. Quinn would be sitting with his family.

"Ingrid!" Deidre hailed her from inside her barn owl costume. "Glad you made it, girlfriend!"

"Wouldn't miss it! Love the costume!"

"Hey, Ingrid!" Jo was decked out as a falcon. "What a trouper you are!"

"Hi, Jo!" To calm her nerves, she focused on the Whine and Cheese ladies in their spectacular costumes. On the far side of the room, the magnificent bald eagle must be Christine, who had the height to carry it off. Judy was perfect as a pygmy owl. "Kendra, these costumes are *amazing.*"

"We're so proud of them. They'll get lots of use, too. We'll wear them for every Raptors Rise event." She paused next to a circular table for eight. "Hey, everybody! Look who's here."

Ingrid pasted on a big smile and did a fast sweep of the table—Roxanne, Luke and Abigail, Quinn, Pete, Gage...and Wes. *Breathe.*

Everyone started talking at once, mostly asking about her health. She assured them she was fine. After some shifting of seats, Quinn positioned her between Roxanne and Abigail. Quinn held the chair and scooted her in.

"Thank you." She glanced over her shoulder and smiled at him. When she faced forward, Wes was directly across from her.

He cleared his throat. "Glad you're better."

"Thanks."

He held her gaze. *I won't let you down. Ever.* Then Gage said something and he turned to respond.

She was still staring at him when Roxanne wrapped an arm around her and gave her a quick squeeze. "I'm so glad you've recovered. I was worried about you. You hardly ever get sick."

"I know. I—" She was interrupted when Deidre arrived to take her order.

"Bear with me," Deidre's wings fluttered as she poked at the touchscreen of the digital order tablet. "I can't fit my glasses under the headpiece and I haven't figured out how to enlarge the print on this thing."

"I can enlarge it for you." Roxanne held out her hand.

"Excellent." Deidre gave her the tablet. "I should've asked you earlier. Then I wouldn't have scrambled that lady's order."

Ingrid glanced up at her. "What happened?"

"She wanted ginger ale and I brought her gin and tonic by mistake. But she drank it right down and seemed happy with it. In fact, she asked for another one."

Roxanne grinned. "See? No worries. Want me to take Ingrid's order while I'm at it?"

"Thanks. I suck at this, Ingrid, but can you please give me a humongous tip, anyway? We're donating all our tips to Raptors Rise."

"I absolutely will." She chose something at random from the abbreviated menu, doubting she'd eat a bite of it. "And I *do* want ginger ale, please."

Roxanne entered the order and handed the tablet back to Deidre. "That's what you'll get. Alcohol would be a bad idea after what you've been through."

So true.

Kendra hurried over and grabbed Deidre by the wing. "Get that order in pronto. When Nicole and Bryce finish this song, we're going to do the thing."

"Hot damn. Now that part I *am* good at." She glanced at Quinn. "You're up first, though. C'mon."

"I'm on it." He pushed back his chair. "If you'll all excuse me."

"Go get 'em, Dad," Rox said.

Ingrid leaned toward her. "What's happening?"

"He and Zane will unveil the picture and talk about Raptors Rise. And after that...well, you'll just have to wait and see. We need to turn our chairs around."

Ingrid was only too happy to oblige. Sooner or later someone was bound to notice that she kept glancing at Wes.

Bryce and Nicole finished their number with a flourish and Bryce stepped up to the mic. "If you'll all give your attention to my big brother

Zane, he and our resident artist Quinn Sawyer have a treat for you."

Zane and Quinn stood on either side of the large draped picture propped on an easel. Zane lifted the mic in his hand. "When Mandy and I were kids we dreamed of creating a rescue organization to help these noble birds of prey survive and thrive. All this..." He paused to sweep an arm around the room. "An entire community coming together for that cause, proves that dreams can come true. Thank you."

The room erupted in cheers and Zane waited for the hubbub to die down before continuing. "Quinn Sawyer's new to Eagles Nest but he's already contributed so much to this town. He's donating what you're about to see to Raptors Rise. It will hang in the GG for the next month to draw attention to the organization. After that it will have a place of honor in the lobby of our visitor center. Quinn, I can't begin to tell you how grateful I am."

"You're very welcome, Zane." Quinn shook hands with him before taking the mic. "Zane's efforts with Raptors Rise have inspired me from my first visit to Eagles Nest. It certainly inspired this. I call it *Home, Sweet Home*. After tonight, prints and notecards with this image will be for sale in the gift shop and a portion of the proceeds will benefit Raptors Rise." He glanced over at Zane. "Ready?"

Ingrid leaned toward Rox. "This is so exciting," she murmured. "Have you seen it?"

"I have. You'll love it."

Zane and Quinn each grasped a corner of the drape and flipped it backward.

Murmurs and gasps of delight filled the room. Then one of the Sawyer boys—sounded like Wes—called out *Yeah!* and started clapping. Instantly the crowd was on its feet, applauding *Home, Sweet Home*, an image of an eagle family— two chicks tucked in the nest protected by mom's wing while dad stood guard.

Ingrid drew a shaky breath. *Home, Sweet Home.* What a beautiful tribute to the love of family. Quinn believed in it or he wouldn't have created this piece of art.

Wes believed in it, too. He'd demonstrated it time and again in his devotion to his dad, his sister and his brothers. Because of their close bond, he trusted them and they returned the favor.

If he told Roxanne that he was confident his new relationship with Ingrid would work out just fine, she'd trust his judgment. She wouldn't worry about it.

And as that realization dawned, another followed close on its heels. Had it really been Roxanne's feelings she'd been protecting? Or, as Wes had said, was this her issue? Gazing at the eagles, the truth hit her between the eyes.

As the applause died down, Kendra walked over to Quinn. Laughing, he placed a kiss on her beak before handing her the mic.

"Eagles Nesters!" Kendra spread her wings as she sauntered over to the dance floor where her four costumed friends had gathered. "Thanks to the incredible talents of Mandy

Fielding McGavin, the Whine and Cheese Club is appropriately dressed for this..." She glanced at Deidre, who was busy preening her feathers. "What should we call this?"

"It's a happening!"

"Alrighty, then! Let the happening begin!" She set the mic on the nearest table and turned toward the bandstand. "Hit it, kids!"

Bryce and Nicole launched into a rousing country version of *Shake Ya Tailfeather* and the Whine and Cheese ladies threw themselves into a raucous, tush-wiggling dance.

Ingrid laughed until the tears came. She wouldn't have missed this for the world. When the dance ended, she yelled and stomped with everyone else as the tight knot of anxiety slowly loosened. *I won't let you down. Ever.*

"That's it, folks," Kendra was breathless as she grabbed the mic again. "It's time for eating, drinking, and celebrating being a part of this wonderful town. Be kind to your wait staff. We know not what we do."

Rox turned to Ingrid and gave her a hug. "I'm so glad you got over the flu and could come tonight."

Ingrid met her gaze. "I didn't have the flu."

"What?"

"Listen, since the food's not here, yet, could we...can I talk to you outside?"

"Of course."

"It won't take long." She started toward the front door, winding through the tables.

Rox followed close behind. "If you didn't have flu, what's wrong? Is it something worse?"

"It's nothing bad, I promise."

"But you missed work. You don't do that."

"I'll explain." She walked into the cool night air and turned as Rox came through the door. "I'm in love with Wes."

Rox's eyes registered shock. "You're...my brother...Wes? You're in love with Wes?"

"I didn't mean for it to happen, but I'm pretty sure he's in love with me, too. I was worried about telling you this, but—"

"I never in a million years thought—"

"I know." She took a deep breath. "I'm supposed to be on hiatus. That's why I asked him not to tell anyone that we were seeing each other, especially you, but he wasn't happy about keeping it a secret."

Rox scrubbed her fingers through her dark hair. "So when...how long have you..."

"It started last week."

"When last week?"

"Thursday night."

"So on Saturday, when we all watched the movie...?" Her brow scrunched up.

"We were already together."

"Whoa."

"And this is the place where I should be saying I'm sorry. And I am, because I should have told you. I should have trusted you with the information. But I'm not sorry that I've fallen in love with—"

"Wait, wait." She put up both hands. "You're going too fast. Something's not adding up. If you're not sorry you're in love with him, why did you pretend to be sick?"

"That's where it gets complicated."

"It's already complicated! Okay, let's back up. You're in love with my brother. He's not your rebound guy or a passing fancy."

"Absolutely not."

"Do you love him more than you did Mark?"

"Mark's not even in the same league as Wes. I've never felt like this about any guy. I look at him and I want to gobble him up. He's warm and passionate and funny and he really knows how to—"

"TMI. Let's not forget I'm his little sister."

"Right."

"But it's good to hear you talk like that. You never talked like that about Mark."

"I know. And I should've told you about this."

Rox gazed at her. "Maybe, although I can kind of see why you didn't. You figured I'd think it was too soon."

"It *is* really soon, but Wes is amazing. He's perfect for me and I think...I hope...I'm perfect for him."

Rox gazed at her. "The idea's growing on me. I can see how you two would be pretty great together. But I still don't understand the stomach flu thing."

"Yesterday we sort of...broke up."

"Broke *up?* Why, for God's sake? You just said you love him, so—"

"He wanted to tell everybody and go to this event as a couple. I refused. I'd convinced myself that you'd be upset, that I had to protect you from the truth, when in fact, I was protecting myself. And projecting my own fears onto you."

Her expression softened. "You can always tell me the truth."

"I know that, now. It was all about me. I was afraid Wes would hurt me like Mark did, only instead of it happening in Boston, my entire life here in Eagles Nest would be ruined in the process."

"Oh, Ingrid." She enveloped her in a hug. "He would never treat you that way."

"Of course he wouldn't." She drew back and sniffed. "Even if it didn't work out, knowing him, he'd try to take all the blame."

"Yeah, he would."

"Because that's the kind of guy he is, loyal and kind, sweet and considerate. I love him so much, Rox."

"Have you told him that?"

"No."

"If I send him out here, will you promise to tell him?"

She gulped. "Yes."

"Then stay here. I'll go get him."

"Okay. You're a good friend."

"So are you." Rox gave her another quick hug and hurried inside.

Ingrid paced in front of the door until Wes came barreling out.

He stopped in front of her, breathing hard. "You told her."

"I did."

He dragged in air. "And she seems okay with—"

"I love you."

He stared at her.

"You look surprised."

"I didn't...I thought it would take..."

"Time?"

He nodded.

"I thought so, too." She stepped closer. "I was wrong. I started falling in love with you when you scooped me up and carried me over the finish line of the three-legged race. But I was scared to admit it. I was afraid..."

"That I'd hurt you?"

"Yes. I didn't trust you, even though everything you've said and done has been telling me I couldn't find a more trustworthy guy than you."

"Or one who loves you more than I do."

Her breath caught.

"I've said this in my head a hundred times." He held her gaze. "Now I get to say it out loud. I love you, Ingrid. And we are going to be so happy together you won't be able to stand it."

She soaked up every bit of warmth in his beautiful eyes. "I believe you."

"That's all I've been waiting to hear." Reaching for her, he drew her gently into his arms. And as he kissed her, the last tiny scrap of fear disappeared from her heart, leaving room for love. So much love.

Epilogue

Although Gage had announced to Wes that he intended to go see the woman in Great Falls, it was several weeks before he climbed in his truck and pointed it in that direction. It was the sort of enterprise that took some mental preparation. Besides, it was fun hanging around Eagles Nest and observing Wes in full love-struck mode.

Their dad was nearly as besotted, but at least he'd had some time to settle into a less manic phase. Wes, on the other hand, could barely get through a conversation without referencing his sweetie-pie. Cute as hell. Gage was happy for him.

Coupling up was all the rage in his family these days. His sis and Michael were nearly finished building their love nest outside of town and had hinted they might be tying the knot soon. Pete was the only sure thing if Gage wanted company for drinking beer on the porch.

He might have procrastinated longer on Project Emma except he'd run out of things to do around his dad's place. Unlike the Lazy S, this operation didn't require much maintenance. While he'd stashed away enough money that he didn't absolutely need a job for another six or eight months, he preferred having satisfying work. The real joy in porch sitting with a beer came after completing a long day of honest labor.

But he'd postponed job-hunting until he found out whether Emma had any interest in picking up where they'd left off. That might not seem logical to anyone else, but it did to him. And now it was time to make the trip to Great Falls.

He chose to drive up on a weekday. He'd arrive about four and if she had the same job, bartending at a cozy little Western place he used to frequent, she wouldn't have started her shift yet. If she wasn't at her house, he'd try the bar.

Just showing up was a little crazy and he owned that. He'd always tended to color outside the lines. He figured if it was supposed to work out between them, she'd be at home. After the first shock, she'd be glad to see him. She'd invite him in and they'd...take it from there.

The closer he got to Great Falls, the more he wanted it to happen that way. The timing had been wrong a year and a half ago but it might be perfect now. A Christmas romance had been a dicey concept from the get-go. Sentimental songs, meaningful gifts and mistletoe kisses just confused the issue.

If he ended up staying the night, he'd text Pete and let him know. And if he spent the night.... Probably shouldn't contemplate that. Not while he was behind the wheel.

But just saying he did stay tonight, then what? Shouldn't he have some sort of game plan? Some path forward?

Factors to consider—he'd become fond of Eagles Nest. Reconnecting with his family had been awesome. He wouldn't mind making Eagles Nest his home base.

Last time he'd been in Great Falls, Emma hadn't seemed totally bonded with the town. Didn't have family close by. She'd said something about road-tripping with a girlfriend and ending up there. The friend had left but Emma had landed a job and hadn't gone with her.

He couldn't imagine her not liking Eagles Nest, though, and business was booming at the Guzzling Grizzly. He'd considered asking for a job there. But he wasn't ready to tie himself down to anything. Not yet.

First he had to settle this thing with Emma. It was the first step in creating a different life than the rolling stone existence he'd maintained for years, ever since driving away from the Lazy S at eighteen.

He was slightly jacked up on adrenaline when he turned onto her street. He'd been singing along with a country station but he switched that off.

The neighborhood looked a lot different from the last time he'd been there—no Christmas lights, no snow on the ground. Grass and leafed-out trees, instead. A couple of bikes were propped against a garage door at one house, and a woman at the place next door was watering her shrubs with a hose. She gave him a curious glance.

Emma's house, a tidy one-story rental with white clapboard siding and a small covered porch, was on his left. He continued past it and checked for her vehicle. His pulse rate picked up. There was her gray SUV, sitting in the driveway.

His throat felt like a weathered fence post. Should've brought a jug of water. Hands were a bit shaky, too. Not how he wanted to present himself.

Her street turned into a dead end, so he swung his truck around and sat for a minute, gathering his courage. Damn, his heart was going fast, too fast.

Back in Eagles Nest, this moment had seemed like a slam dunk. All he'd have to do was park his truck, jog up the steps to her porch, ring the doorbell, tip his hat and flash her a big smile.

Okay. It was still a good plan. He just had to execute. Dragging in air, he put the truck in gear. Show time.

He parked in front of her house instead of in her driveway, in case she had to leave for work soon. Would she hear his truck and look out the window? She used to say she recognized the sound of it coming down the street.

Heart pounding, he shut off the engine, picked up his hat from the passenger seat and climbed out. He shoved his keys in his pocket, took another deep breath and started up her walk.

He repositioned his hat at a better angle before mounting the steps and crossing the porch. He jabbed the bell way harder than necessary because his hands were still shaking, damn it.

The light, quick footsteps inside the house were hers. Funny how he was so sure of it after all this time, but she had a certain pace to her walk.

She opened the door. Her green eyes widened and her pretty mouth went slack.

Without makeup, she looked sixteen instead of twenty-six.

He didn't give her a jaunty smile or throw out a casual greeting like he'd planned. All he could do was stare. She was the same but different.

Her taffy-colored hair, so silky when he'd combed his fingers through it, was shorter. It barely touched her shoulders. She wore jeans and a tank top instead of jeans and a sweater. Her feet were bare, her toenails unpolished.

Her beauty made his chest ache. What an idiot he'd been.

She swallowed. "Gage."

"Hi, Emma."

"What...what are you doing here?"

"Came to see you." His vocal cords weren't working quite right.

"Why?"

"Been thinking about you. I've thought about you a lot ever since—"

"Did you try to contact me? Because I never got anything."

"I didn't. I should've, but I didn't."

"Are you back in Great Falls?"

"No, I'm living about three hours south of here, a little town called Eagles Nest."

"So why did you come up here?"

"Like I said, to see you. You've been on my mind."

"You drove up here just to see me?"

"Yes, and I—could I come in?"

"Uh..." Panic flashed in her eyes.

"No big deal. I just want to talk for a bit."

Her jaw tightened. "Now's not a good time."

"Are you working tonight? If that's the problem, I could—"

"I'm...I don't...my circumstances have changed." She was breathing fast. "I don't want to talk right now."

"When?"

"The thing is, I don't want to talk at all. I need you to...go. Please leave."

"Hey, if you're with somebody, you can just tell me."

"Goodbye, Gage. I'm sorry you came up here for nothing."

"But—"

"Goodbye." She closed the door and the lock clicked into place.

What the hell? In all his dealings with women, he'd been yelled at a few times, slapped once, which he'd absolutely deserved, but no woman had ever closed the door in his face. And *locked* it.

Geez Louise. He wasn't a vagrant off the street. They'd been lovers. They'd had some great times together.

She hadn't been angry, though. Evidently she didn't have another guy. Sure, he hadn't come to see her for nineteen months, but that didn't seem to be the problem.

She just wanted him out of her sight. Out of her life. Whatever they'd had before clearly meant nothing to her anymore.

That was rejection with a capital R, rejection on steroids, rejection in neon lights. It stung worse than the time he'd stumbled into a hornet's nest.

To think he'd pictured Emma as part of the future he was building. Clearly he needed to recalibrate that fantasy. Tugging the brim of his hat down, he stomped back to his truck.

Although gunning the engine and peeling out would have suited him fine, this was a peaceful neighborhood. He drove away at a sedate speed, but once he was back on the highway he punched it. He couldn't get away from her fast enough.

Smooth-talking cowboy Gage Sawyer's speechless when Emma Green arrives in Eagles Nest with his baby in A COWBOY'S BABY, book eleven in the McGavin Brothers series!

* * * * *

When Gage returned to the living room, Emma had put Josh down. He was slowly working his way around the coffee table, his steps determined, his concentration intense.

Gage followed his progress, mesmerized by each wobbly step taken in impossibly tiny gym shoes. His baby was almost walking. His wispy blond hair had a slight curl to it, like Emma's.

"He still needs to hold onto something. But soon he won't have to."

He glanced over at her. She was watching the baby as intently as he was.

Just then the little guy lost his balance. He sat down with a soft thud and a very adult-sounding *oh*.

"Whoops." Gage started toward him, ready to help.

"Let him do it."

"But—"

"This table is a lot like the one I have at home. He can get back up."

Sure enough, the kid shifted to a crawling position, motored back to the table leg and used it to haul himself upright again.

"Smart little guy."

"Oh, yeah. I've baby-proofed the heck out of my house and he still gets into things."

"Were you ever going to tell me?"

Her expression grew wary. "Well, I…" She paused and drew in a shaky breath. "Would you please sit down?"

"Okay." He took the easy chair since he figured she'd rather have him there than cozied up next to her on the sofa. Laying his hat on the arm of the chair, he sat back and waited.

Instead of looking at him, she focused on Josh. "I kept meaning to call you. Well, after I faced the fact I was pregnant."

"I swear I'd just bought those condoms."

"I know. I was the one who opened the box, remember?" She gave him a quick glance before returning her attention to Josh. Her cheeks were pinker than they'd been a moment ago. "It was a fluke."

"Yes, ma'am." Evidently discussing their former sexual activities got to her. It got to him, too, but he'd keep a lid on it. Her first reaction to seeing him again had spoken louder than words. "You still had my number?"

"I never deleted it from my phone. At first I put off calling you because I was in denial. Then I couldn't figure out what to say. In the end, I decided you'd be better off not knowing. You didn't seem like the daddy type, so why throw a monkey-wrench into your life when I didn't expect to ever see you again?"

"And you didn't. Until yesterday."

Turning her head, she met his gaze. "We'd agreed we were just having fun, nothing serious."

"True." Yet those nights with her stood out in vivid detail all these months later. "So if I hadn't come to see you yesterday…"

"You'd be none the wiser."

His chest tightened. Finding out about Josh had knocked him six ways to Sunday, but never finding out….

"Anyway, you did come to see me."

"And you told me to leave."

"I wasn't prepared. I panicked. I had no idea how you'd react."

"You didn't know how I'd react today, either, but you still brought him down. Why?"

"Because seeing you again and not telling you felt like a lie. I couldn't make that decision for you again. You deserved to know."

He regarded her silently. Bringing the baby down here had taken courage. "Thank you."

Some of the tension eased from her expression. "You're welcome."

"What now?"

"I guess…we need to talk about it. But please understand that I don't expect anything from you. You deserve to know, but you don't have any responsibility, here. You're free to go on with your life as if Josh and I don't exist."

He stared at her. "Are you kidding?"

"Not at all." Her expression gentled. "You didn't choose this, Gage. I don't want to saddle you with a child you never intended to create."

"You didn't choose this either."

"Not initially, but after I made my decision, I never looked back. I haven't regretted it for one second. You had no say, though. Expecting you to adjust your life to fit a choice I made is unfair."

He met her gaze. "I don't know what's fair or unfair. This is all so..."

"You're still in shock."

"Yeah." He scrubbed a hand through his hair. "That about sums it up. I need some...time."

She nodded.

"But I can tell you one thing."

"What's that?"

"I could never go on with my life as if you and Josh didn't exist."

*New York Times bestselling author Vicki Lewis
Thompson's love affair with cowboys started with
the Lone Ranger, continued through Maverick, and
took a turn south of the border with Zorro. She
views cowboys as the Western version of knights in
shining armor, rugged men who value honor,
honesty and hard work. Fortunately for her, she
lives in the Arizona desert, where broad-shouldered,
lean-hipped cowboys abound. Blessed with such an
abundance of inspiration, she only hopes that she
can do them justice.*

*For more information about this prolific author,
visit her website and sign up for her newsletter. She
loves connecting with readers.*

VickiLewisThompson.com